Twits on the Hunt

A Steampunk Distraction

Tom Alan Robbins

BOOK FIVE OF THE TWITS CHRONICLES

Claim A Free Gift!

Visit Twitschronicles.com to claim a free copy of the Twits short story *Uncle Hugo's Crisis.* Or, if you are reading this on a device, you can click HERE.

What People Are Saying:

"The Twits Chronicles are hilarious, blessed with truly exceptional dialogue. Steampunk dystopia meets Oscar Wildean wit in these books. I found myself laughing out loud on numerous occasions--and that's not something I often do while reading. "

—Nick Sullivan, author of The Deep Series and Zombie Bigfoot.

"Delightful! A frothy frappe of P.G. Wodehouse and steam-punk. If you're the sort who reads blurbs before reading the book, stop it. Stop it right now. Read TWITS IN LOVE and have a good time. These days we can all use a bit more of a good time."

—John Ostrander, American writer of comic books, including *Suicide Squad, Grimjack* and *Star Wars: Legacy*.

"I haven't enjoyed the company of such eccentric characters since A Confederacy of Dunces, and Tom Alan Robbins has managed to place them in the stylized world of Oscar Wilde. A really unique journey."

— Kevin Conroy, Actor, The voice behind the DC Comics superhero Batman .

"Tom Alan Robbins' Twits stories are hilarious, thought provoking and mind bending. His juicy turns of phrase will stick in your ear like a catchy song."

— Michael Urie, Actor, Producer and Director

"Tom is the most talented, delicious writer. Do yourself a favor, and immerse yourself in the fabulous world of TWITS!"

— Mary Testa, 3 time Tony Award Nominee

Cover design by Melody J. Barber of Aurora Publicity

Additional designs by Eric Wright of The Puppet Kitchen.

Twits Logo designed by Feppa Rodriquez

Proofreading by Gretchen Tannert Douglas

For Bob, who taught me how to tie a tie and who has excelled at being my big brother for more years than either of us cares to admit to.
To my superlative sister-in-law Melinda and my astonishing nieces and nephew: Julia, Catherine, Caroline and Eli.

Steampunk

"Steampunk is a subgenre of science fiction that incorporates retrofuturistic technology and aesthetics inspired by 19th-century industrial steam-powered machinery. Steampunk works are often set in an alternative history of the Victorian era or the American "Wild West", where steam power remains in mainstream use, or in a fantasy world that similarly employs steam power."

Wikipedia

A Word About Timelines

For those who are unfamiliar with the Steampunk genre, a word about timelines may be helpful. The Steampunk Universe in which The Twits Chronicles take place is clearly not our own. That is why events and cultural references that happened in vastly different eras in our own world seem to happen in a compressed time period. It feels as if we are in a vaguely Victorian era, and yet there are references to events and quotations from well into the twentieth century.

It may help to think of this as an exercise in "what if?" What if electricity wasn't discovered until much later in human history? Human ingenuity would still search for new ways of using existing technology, and so steam power and mechanical engineering would keep advancing, while much of the aesthetic of the world around us could remain in the nineteenth century.

The world that would result is the world of *The Twits Chronicles*. Other writers would use these same criteria to create very different realities. This is mine.

Enter and enjoy.

Contents

CHAPTER ONE

The Chase Begins

Time, it has always seemed to me, is not the linear, inflexible creature that railroad timetables would have us believe. It has a caramel-like quality that can stretch endlessly on a Sunday afternoon. On this particular Sunday it had clearly lost all motivation and flopped around the house sighing and flipping through old magazines, so it was a positive relief when Bentley wafted in on a breeze to inform me that my chinless cousin, Cheswick Wickford-Davies (Binky, to his friends) was in the front hallway doing something odd.

Bentley, as I'm sure you are aware, is my mechanical valet. His origins are shrouded in the mists of time, but he has been with the family for generations and his loyalty and resourcefulness are beyond question.

"What do you mean, odd? Odder than usual?"

"I would describe his manner as furtive, Sir. He is standing by a window in the entryway and peeping through the curtains."

"Better see what it's about, then."

I trundled off to the front hallway, where I found Binky engaged in the aforementioned peeping. He was crouched next to a preserved walrus that had been harpooned by my great-great grandfather, Percy. Alas, this proud pinniped would never have a mate stuffed and mounted by his side. Since The Great Extinction, walruses had joined the rhinoceros and the zebu in that great menagerie in the sky.

I peered over his shoulder to see what he was staring at. "Hallo, Old Boot! What's it all about?"

He shrieked and leaped into the air. Holding a hand to his heart he stared at me as he slid slowly down the wall to sit on the marble tiles. He gestured for me to hang on for a tick and laboured to slow his breathing. Bentley and I watched him carefully.

"Shall I fetch my medical kit, Sir?"

I leaned over and shouted in Binky's ear. "Do you want some drugs, Old Sot?"

He shook his head and made a superhuman effort to speak. "No! No, I'm all right. Just let me sit here for a moment."

"Sorry if I startled you."

"It wasn't your fault. I'm a bit on edge."

"So I see. Live free or die."

"Live free or die. Could you take a peek out front and see if there's anyone lurking about?"

"Only too glad." I parted the curtains and gave the street the once over. "Nothing untoward that I can see. Just a young person cleaning her nails with a knife."

"What? Help me up!"

"She can't be more than eight! You're not frightened of a child!"

"That's why she's so dangerous! No one would suspect her. Give me a hand, will you?"

I hauled him onto his trotters and brushed him down in a general way. He peered out of the window.

"Diabolical," he muttered.

I looked at Bentley inquiringly. He gave a little cough.

"I believe Mr. Wickford-Davies's apprehension stems from a debt of honour."

"What? Oh, yes, a debt of honour without question. It was a sure thing, you know."

I patted him gently on the soft part of his head. "I'm not sure you understand what that phrase actually means, Old Clot."

He slumped. "I've landed myself in the frying pan for good this time and no onions to soften the fall."

I turned to Bentley. "Can you elaborate? The plot is still somewhat murky."

"According to my sources, Mr. Wickford-Davies has lost a rather substantial wager on the outcome of the Annual Delivery Persons' Race."

Binky stared at Bentley in awe but I was used to this omniscience that he trotted out when called upon. The Annual Delivery Persons' Race, for those who have not had the pleasure, is a *fete* organized by my club, Twits. Any member of the Delivery Persons Union is eligible. They race around an obstacle course with their delivery carts and the winner receives a trophy, which is engraved with their name and displayed in a glass case near the club cloakroom. It is not uncommon for large wagers to be placed on the favourites.

"I couldn't lose! Ernie could give the rest of the field twenty metres and still breeze home by a length."

"Ernie? My Head of Research?"

"He still moonlights at his delivery job. Says it offers more opportunity for advancement than scientific experimentation."

"All right, you bet on him and presumably he lost?"

"He was nobbled! Someone loosened the wheels on his cart. They fell off halfway down the course. Even so, he came in second."

"And now you owe money to a shady criminal enterprise?"

"Of course not! The betting for these things is controlled by the government—Bureau of Wagers. Nothing shady about it."

"Then who is following you?"

"Bureau of Collections. Bunch of fanatics. Chop off your thumbs as soon as look at you."

"These hooligans work for the government?"

"Absolutely. Civil Service— pension, benefits... it's a plum job."

"This is ridiculous. How much do you owe them? I'll cover it."

"You will? Bless you, Old Friend."

"Can't have them chopping off your thumbs, what? How would you play bridge?"

"I could be the dummy."

Before I could choose a punchline, Bentley cleared his throat. "Forgive me, Sir, but if my information is correct, you do not have sufficient funds to cover the amount in question."

I stared at him. "How can that be? I'm as rich as Midas."

"You are forgetting that you are on an allowance. The bulk of your wealth is beyond your reach."

"When did that happen?"

"It was a recent occurrence. If you recall, you felt that endless riches leached all the flavour from life. You wished to be relieved of that burden and the solution was to put you on a strict allowance."

I looked at Binky sharply. "How could you bet such an enormous sum?"

"It was a sure thing."

"Stop saying that. Why would they allow you to make such a bet? It must be pretty generally known that you're a sponger of the first water."

He blushed and looked nervously at his toes. "Oh dear, you're going to be cross with me."

"Will I?"

"Yes. You see, I may have put you down as a co-signer on the bet."

"And they took your word?"

"Not exactly. I may have... forged your signature just a teensy bit."

I stared at him in shock. "You did what?"

"It was nothing! You would never have known about it."

"Do you mean I'm on the hook for your losses?"

"I was going to cut you in on the winnings. It was a sure..."

"If you say that again I swear I'll pull you by the nose."

He fell silent and looked at me gloomily. I set to work assimilating all this info into the old grey matter but odd bits kept sliding out of the frame. Finally, I turned to Bentley.

"I'm stumped, Bentley. Should we hand him over to the authorities?"

He gave a little shake of the head. "I'm afraid Mr. Wickford-Davies would not thrive in a prison environment. Perhaps I can find a solution if given a bit of time."

There was a knock on the door. We all stared at it apprehensively.

"What should we do?" I whispered to Bentley. He stepped up to the door and looked through the peephole. A harsh voice spoke from outside.

"I see the shadow on the other side of the peephole. I know you are at home. My name is Mr. Null. I am from the government. I must ask you to open the door."

Bentley turned to us. His gears ground away for a moment and he turned back to the door. "Mr. Chippington-Smythe is not at home, Sir. I have strict instructions not to admit anyone in his absence."

The voice took on a sarcastic tone. "And I suppose that wasn't Cheswick Wickford-Davies that went through this very door not five minutes ago?"

A high, piping voice joined in from the front stoop. "He's in there all right, Da. I saw him myself."

"That's a good lass, Daisy. You play with your knife and later we'll get ice cream." The voice addressed us through the door again. "Your employer is co-signer on a very large wager that is now due. He and Mr. Wickford-Davies must come up with the cash forthwith or suffer the consequences."

Bentley turned to us. "I believe the best course of action is an evasive maneuver. I suggest that you depart over the garden wall and make your way to the club, where the law has no power to follow you. I shall keep Mr. Null and his daughter engaged in conversation while you make good your escape."

"Right-oh, Bentley. Come by later with an update, will you?"

"I should be able to formulate a plan of action by then, Sir."

Turning to the door he cleared his throat. "May I ask you to repeat your name, Sir?"

"Null! N, U, L, L. I'm from the Bureau of Collections."

Binky and I didn't wait to hear more. We scampered back to the garden. There was a ladder lying by the wall from an earlier escapade and we hastily hauled it upright and climbed over into the garden of the house behind me. This house, I had recently learned, was occupied by an aged nymphomaniac named Madame Sallope who, in her younger days, was known for sleeping with the entire resident company of the Comedie Francaise, including the props mistress and the mime who handed out the playbills. To my horror, she lay sunning herself beside the hydrangeas and had watched us climb into her yard with great interest.

"Ah, good morning, Madame! Live free or die. Forgive the intrusion. Bit of a problem with the front door. Termites, I'm told. Had to use the back exit. Be out of your way instantly. Please don't get up."

Alas, she had already risen to her feet and came swaying toward us with a lascivious gleam in her eye.

"Not at all, *chéri*! I wish beautiful young men would climb into my garden more often. Live free or die. It is Monsieur Chippington-Smythe, *n'est-ce pas?*"

I dredged up what little French I could remember from my school days.

"*Oui. Est* this is *mon cousin*, Cheswick Wickford-Davies."

Binky popped in a "Live free or die."

"*Alors*, at last we meet! It is a great pleasure. May I offer you a Pernod? Or an absinthe?"

I was about to make our excuses when Binky, ignoring my warning look, sang out, "What's an absinthe?"

The old girl gave a kittenish giggle. "The green fairy! Come, follow me."

Binky stepped out smartly and I had no choice but to follow him. Madame Sallope led us through some French doors and into a sort of Moorish seraglio. There was a glass and copper contraption on a table with a pitcher full of green liquid underneath it. Water was dripping onto a glucose cube in a little holder and from there into the pitcher. She neatly tipped the solution into a couple of glasses without spilling a drop and handed them over.

"This is the true absinthe that inspired so many great artists. *À votre santé*!"

Well, a drink is a drink. I tipped my head back and poured it down the old sluice. Despite its cheery green colour, it was powerful stuff. I grabbed the back of a chair to keep myself upright and breathed shallowly until the burning sensation had eased. Before I could regain the power of speech Madame Sallope filled my glass again. I dutifully downed it and noticed that it barely burned this time. Binky was sipping at his third go round. A pleasant warmth began in my toes.

"I say, this stuff is just the thing. Surprised I never had it before."

"Oh, it is illegal in this country. I have a friend who acquires it for me."

"Illegal? Why, what's in it?"

"The secret ingredient is wormwood. Some say it causes hallucinations. It is also rumoured to be an aphrodisiac. Of course such claims are ridiculous..."

"You don't say."

"...So, I am forced to add my own special concoction of *actual* aphrodisiacs to the drink."

"What?"

"*Ooh la la*! It is so hot in here, *n'est-ce pas*? Why not take off your shirts?"

The room was rather steamy. I hadn't noticed it before. Binky was mopping his face with a handkerchief. The perspiration was pouring off of him.

"That's a sensible idea. I feel like a prize orchid in this tropical heat."

He actually reached for a button before I grabbed his elbow.

"Perhaps another time. Thanks awfully for the drinks. Afraid we must run. Enterprises of great pith and moment and all that. Ta-ta!"

And with that I seized Binky and dragged him into the open air. I could hear Madame Sallope crying, "Wait, wait!" behind us but I soldiered on until we were safely down the road.

Chapter Two

Momentary Refuge

Binky shook off my grip and looked at me reproachfully.

"That was rude. She was trying to be neighbourly. Sweet old thing."

"She was trying to drug us! Another drink and we would have been rolling about on the carpet in our underwear!"

He looked back at her mansion wistfully. "I'm sure her intentions were honourable."

"How many of those things did you drink?"

"I don't know. Three or four. They went down pretty fast."

"Well get hold of yourself. It's a long way to the club. Must be at least four blocks. Perhaps you'll walk it off."

We trudged down the road, keeping a sharp lookout for Mr. Null and his daughter, but we arrived in front of "Twits" without incident. The protesters were there as usual. My eye was drawn to a large sign that bore the slogan, "Eat the Rich."

"Is there a cannibalism movement I'm unaware of?"

Binky's spirits revived. "My insolvency is an asset at last. I'm too poor to be eaten."

"I doubt that they'll wait to check your bank balance before chucking you in the stew pot, Old Roast. You *look* rich and that means you're on the menu."

Scouting the vicinity, I spied my nemesis Cubby Martinez, the Marshall of Twits, crossing the square escorting a young lady. Suddenly I recognized her—it was Cubby's stepsister, Euphonia Gumboot! We had left her in New York after a recent adventure and she had expressed her intention to remain there forever. Forever, however, was a malleable concept for Euphonia since she lacked a short-term memory. As they drew close Cubby pretended not to see us. I waved enthusiastically.

"Hallo, Euphonia! How nice to see you again. Live free or die."

She stared at me blankly. "I don't believe I've had the pleasure."

I chuckled. "Of course, you wouldn't remember. I'm Cyril Chippington-Smythe. You rode over to New York in my dirigible."

"I have never been to New York," she demurred.

Cubby held up a warning hand. "Please do not agitate my sister, Chippington-Smythe. She has only just arrived after a bit of trouble in the Colonies. She wishes to be left in peace."

Euphonia wrinkled her brow. "Was there trouble? I'm sure it was a misunderstanding."

Cubby turned to her soothingly. "It wasn't your fault. Because of your condition, you are incapable of taking an ambiguous position on any issue that arises. We should have known that a public figure in America who fails to obfuscate their answers cannot survive for long."

I looked at him in amazement. "Are the Americans really so delicate that a simple answer drives them into a frenzy."

Cubby grunted. "You have no idea! The factions there are so at odds with each other that no matter what answer one gives, one is certain to enrage a good part of the population. Poor Euphonia could not remember to cloak her answers in ambivalence. At the end, mobs that were diametrically opposed to one another could only agree that my sister must be deported or clapped into prison. We took the next ship for home."

Binky had been inching toward Euphonia all this while with his eyes as big as saucers. "I don't suppose you remember me? I'm Binky."

"Are you? I'm sorry."

"No, it's my name."

"That is not your fault, then. Your parents are to blame."

"You're looking awfully well, Euphonia. America must have been good for you."

"One moment, if you don't mind."

Euphonia reached for a small notebook that hung around her neck by a cord. She drew out a tiny pencil and squinted at the opened page. "What did you say your name was?"

"Binky"

"Spell it, please."

He did so and she made a note in her little book. "If we meet again, you are on page sixteen. Simply remind me and I can look you up."

"How ingenious! You are as clever as you are lovely."

I glanced sharply at Binky. His pupils had expanded to the size of manhole covers and a fine sheen of perspiration coated his upper lip. Clearly he was still in the grip of Madame Sallope's concoction. For that matter, Euphonia was beginning to look surprisingly appealing to me as well. Binky dug a toe into the ground and peeped at her shyly.

"I say, Euphonia... that is... I don't suppose you'd want to have dinner with me this evening?"

Cubby put a protective arm around his sister. "She would not."

Euphonia removed his arm. "I can speak for myself, Cubby." She smiled at Binky. "I would love to. This evening, you said?" She leafed through her little notebook. "I am free in one hour. When you call for me remind me that our engagement is on page sixteen."

"I am the happiest of men," swooned Binky. He reached for her hand and readied his lips to give it a good coat of varnish but Cubby intercepted him.

"You can have dinner in the club dining room. I shall provide a pass for Euphonia. That way I can keep an eye on you."

Euphonia smacked him playfully. "What a poop you are, Cubby."

Binky retreated, never taking his eyes off of Euphonia. "I would accede to the most outrageous demands in order to spend an evening with a woman of such unparalleled grace and beauty." He was breathing heavily through his nostrils and I watched him for signs of hyperventilation.

"Oh, la, Mr. Wickford-Davies! I shall have to add a note about you in my little book." She scribbled for a moment, glancing up at Binky and nibbling on her lower lip.

Cubby squirmed. "Come, Euphonia, I must go in to work. You may stroll about the dress shop until dinner. I shall tie you to the changing room door with a ribbon as usual and call for you in one hour."

Euphonia checked an entry in her book and frowned. "Please make sure the ribbon is long enough to reach the Summer frocks. I was brought up short last time and it was most vexing."

Binky capered and whinnied. "I can accompany Miss Gumboot! There will be no need for fetters with me in attendance."

I grabbed his arm. "Afraid it's not on the menu, Old Spoon. Inside, quick!"

I had spotted Mr. Null and his daughter entering the square. The young lady pointed at us and yelled to her father. He began to race toward us, pulling what looked like a blackjack out of his pocket. I seized Binky and dragged him up the steps to the entrance of Twits. Evans, the doorman, had seen us coming and quickly opened the door. We fell into the lobby, gasping with relief. Mr. Null stopped on the top step and glared at us. Evans stepped in front of him.

"May I help you, Sir?"

Mr. Null looked at him sourly. "No, I don't suppose I'd get any help from you." He spat on the ground. "Enjoy your stay, gentlemen. You can't hide in there forever." He turned on his heel and was gone. Daisy stood for a moment, frowning at us thoughtfully and flipping her knife from hand to hand, then whirled and set off after her father crying out for ice cream.

I should explain, for those unfamiliar with the history of Twits, that when the club was founded it was declared a place of sanctuary where the laws of the land were suspended. Since most of the founding members were robber barons who had stripped the country of every asset they could lay their hands on, this may have seemed rather self-serving but since these same robber barons were, to a man, members of the ruling party of the time, there was no one to raise an objection. In days of old there were luxurious suites in the club where millionaires on the lam could live out their days in comfort. Most of them had been turned into offices and private dining rooms, but it was rumoured that one of the remaining apartments contained a wizened gentleman who had been evading the law for going on seventy years and who never left his rooms.

Binky and I picked ourselves up and checked for broken bones. Evans brought out a whisk broom and brushed us down.

"A perilous adventure, Sirs. You seem to have come through relatively intact."

"Yes, thank you, Evans. It was a near thing. That Null fellow is a sprinter."

"We have had dealings with him in the past. He is dogged in his pursuits." Evans looked at Binky coolly. "The sponsors of the Annual Delivery Persons' Race would like to have a word with you at your convenience, Sir."

"What, with me? What have I done?"

"There have been accusations of irregularities during the race and yours was the largest wager by far. They wish to satisfy themselves that you had no part in any nobbling that might have occurred."

"Me? I lost a fortune on that race! Do they think I cheated so that I could be chucked into debtor's prison?"

"It is merely an informal inquiry, Sir. They are in the conference room."

Binky sagged and a sigh escaped him. "What a bother. Wait for me, won't you? I'm sure this won't take long."

He moped across the lobby just as Ernie, my Head of Research at Smythe Corporation, came out of the conference room door.

I waved him over. "Ernie! Bad luck about the race! What's all this about dirty dealings at the track?"

He looked distraught. "I don't know how it happened, Sir. I feel responsible. I should have checked my cart before the race began. I don't care so much about losing, but it's put Mr. Wickford-Davies in a terrible spot."

"Never fear. Bentley is on the case. He'll figure out something. You're all in one piece, though?"

"Oh yes. I landed in a bale of straw at the side of the course. I can't imagine who would do such a thing."

"'Who knows what weevils lurk in the hearts of men,' eh? Chewing away at the moral foundations of society like the agricultural pests they once were. I understand you came in second despite your mishap. Well done."

"I'm afraid a miss is as good as a mile in this case, Sir."

There was a flurry of activity and a chorus of "Baaas" from the front entrance as C. Langford-Cheeseworth made his entrance followed by his pet sheep, Compton. I had met Compton (an out-of-work actor who now hired himself out as a pet) on an earlier adventure. I was amused to see that he had been joined by a female in a voluminous ewe costume and a young person impersonating a lamb. Cheeseworth carried a shepherd's crook decorated with a large pink bow. He herded the sheep into the lobby.

"Hallo, Cheeseworth. The flock is growing, I see. Live free or die."

"Cywil! Live fwee or die. Yes, I felt that Compton must be lonely without the company of others of his species, so I hired two more. Say hello, Compton."

Compton pushed the wool out of his eyes and looked up at me. "Baaa, Sir. How nice to see you again."

"Still haven't landed an acting role I see."

"Oh, I've given that up and gone into the pet business full time, Sir. The salary and benefits are ever so much better than the acting game. I've even got my wife and my son in the business now. Say hello, everyone."

The female sheep trotted over but the lamb rolled over on his back and stared at the ceiling sadly.

"This is my wife, Constance."

"How d'you do, Sir? Baa."

"And that over there is Freddy, our boy. Come say hello, Fred."

"Don't want to."

Compton looked at me apologetically. "Boys, Sir. Willful."

Freddy scratched at an itch under his pelt. "Don't want to be a sheep."

"You settle down there, young man. You don't know how lucky you are, getting a start like this. Plenty of lads would give their eye teeth..."

Cheeseworth finally ran out of patience and began laying about him with his crook. The family scattered, bleating for all they were worth.

"Bad sheep! Ungwateful sheep! One more word and I'll turn you into lamb chops." He turned to me apologetically. "I don't know what's gotten into them. They're usually as placid as one could desire."

Binky came moping out of the conference room.

"What ho, Old Sock. What was the verdict?"

"Oh, they didn't really suspect me. I'm the victim, after all."

Cheeseworth patted him sympathetically on the arm. "Poor fellow. I heard all about it. Wuined! Positively wuined! Without funds I suppose you'll be stwipped of your membership."

Binky looked at him in horror. "What? I hadn't considered that! Without my membership I won't be entitled to sanctuary. They'll chuck me out in the square and Null and his daughter can go at me with knives and blackjacks to their hearts' delight."

I gripped his shoulder reassuringly. "Don't you worry. Bentley will come to the rescue. You'll walk out the front door a free man by dinnertime— speaking of which, I'm ravenous."

Binky perked up at once. "I'll join you."

"You're having dinner with Euphonia."

"Am I?"

"You are. Come sit with me until she arrives. Will you join us, Cheeseworth?"

"I'm afwaid they don't allow pets. Enjoy your dinner."

We strolled into the dining room where Rodgers, the Maître d' held sway.

"Good afternoon, Rodgers. Have you got a free table?"

He gave Binky the fish eye. "Will Mr. Wickford-Davies be joining you, Sir?"

"No, he'll be dining with Euphonia Gumboot."

Binky looked at me vaguely. "Are you sure?"

"I am."

Rodgers was still focused on Binky. "On whose account will you be dining, Sir?"

Binky looked wounded. "You wouldn't cut me off, Rodgers?"

"Rules are rules, Sir."

I waved a hand airily. "Put him on my tab. He's my guest today."

"Very good, Sir."

Rodgers led us to a table in the least desirable part of the dining room and strode away with a sniff. Binky watched him go with a morose expression on his mug.

"I've know Rodgers all of my life. How could he be so unfeeling?"

"Robot, you know. The very definition of unfeeling."

My old friends Ford and Lincoln were wending their way toward us.

"Hallo, chaps. Pull up a stool. Live free or die."

They hunched down conspiratorially.

"Live free or die. Well, this is a scandal of monumental proportions," Ford murmured, looking around the room.

Lincoln poked Binky in the arm a few times. "Holding up, Old Fellow? Nasty bit of business if you don't mind my saying. Who do you think it was?"

Binky thought for a moment. "Do you know, I haven't a clue. I don't know who would want to injure me so badly. I've never hurt a fly."

"Detectives in books always say, *'Cherchez la femme,'*" Ford observed.

Binky shook his head. "There's no *femme* in the picture as far as the eye can see. I've been living like a monk."

I waved a fork in his face. "I don't know about that. You were pitching the woo pretty hard at Euphonia out front."

He looked confused. "Isn't that strange? My recollection is rather hazy."

"You'd better sharpen up. She'll be here any moment."

"Will she? I wonder what I was thinking."

Ford gave him an elbow to the side. "You dog! Euphonia Gumboot, eh? Well, each to his own taste."

Binky was growing paler by the moment. "Did I really invite her to dinner?"

"And in front of Cubby too," I observed. "No backing out with his beady little eyes on you."

"Why didn't you stop me?"

"My lad, you would have run me down to get at her. Do you know what I think?"

"No, what?"

"I think you were under the influence of those drinks Madame Sallope poured into us."

"Well, they've worn off now. How am I going to get out of it?"

Ford and Lincoln stared at him disapprovingly.

"You invited the girl, after all."

"One doesn't shirk one's responsibilities."

"You can't just scamper off."

Binky's eyes were turning red. "What a beastly day this has turned into."

Rodgers paced through the dining room with his gong. He gave it a sharp tap and it reverberated among the diners.

"'Neither a borrower nor a lender be.' William Shakespeare." He rapped the gong again. "'The greatest advantage in gambling lies in not playing at all.' Gerolamo Cardano." This time he really put his back into it. "'By gaming we lose both our time and treasure—two things most precious to the life of man.' Owen Feltham."

Binky waved him over. "I say, Rodgers, I can't help but feel that these pronouncements are directed at me."

"I am sorry if you feel that way, Sir. The script for the dining room presentations is chosen far in advance. It must be a coincidence."

"Ah. Yes, it must be."

"Although if it resonates with you perhaps this is an opportunity for some personal growth, Sir."

Binky looked around in anguish. "Why does everyone act like this is my fault? I'm the victim."

I gave his arm a brotherly squeeze and handed over my menu. "Cheesy eggs for me, Rodgers."

"Very good, Sir."

"I say, Rodgers?"

"Sir?"

"Real eggs?"

"Practically, Sir."

"Oh well. Off you go."

Rodgers glided away.

Ford helped himself to a roll. "We should make a list of suspects."

"That's a cracking idea," piped Lincoln. He found a pencil in his pocket and started jotting numbers on the tablecloth. "Who are your enemies?"

Binky looked blank. "I have none."

Ford snorted. "Everyone's got an enemy or two lying around. Any women you've jilted?"

"None that didn't jilt me first."

"Someone you've bested at cards, or sports?"

"I've never come first at anything I've tried."

"Tradespeople you've stiffed?"

"Plenty, but if I go to jail, they'll never get paid."

Lincoln grabbed a roll and looked at him appraisingly. "You might be the most inoffensive person living."

I moved the rolls out of reach. "This is getting us nowhere."

Ford leaned back and chewed for a while. "Perhaps we're going at this from the wrong end. Who stands to benefit from Ernie losing the race?"

This struck me as a sensible question. "I say, if Ernie lost, who won?"

Lincoln frowned. "What was his name?

At that moment I spied Bentley crossing the room at ramming speed. He squealed to a halt by the table and gave a quick little bow. "I am sorry to interrupt your dinner, Sir, but I'm afraid that we must flee."

"Is it so urgent?"

"There is not a moment to be lost. Mr. Wickford-Davies should accompany us as well."

Binky looked up hopefully. "But that means I can't have dinner with Euphonia, doesn't it? Oh well, if Bentley says it's urgent... you all heard him, didn't you? It certainly wasn't my idea, in case Cubby asks."

I jumped to my feet and gave Ford and Lincoln each a quick handshake. "Wish us luck, lads." We cantered toward the exit only to find Euphonia and Cubby blocking the doorway as they made their entrance.

"Here she is, Wickford-Davies," he sneered. "I'll be watching you every moment."

Binky ran a finger around his collar nervously. "Ah, look here Cubby... so sorry Euphonia... as it happens something has come up..."

He got no further. Cubby seized him by the elbow and pulled him roughly to one side. "No, you don't," he hissed. "You invited my sister to dinner and by God you'll provide her with dinner or you'll answer to me."

Bentley leaned in. "If Miss Gumboot will accompany us I can assure you that dinner will be provided for her."

"I'm not letting her out of my sight!"

"In that case, dinner will be provided for you as well."

Euphonia was checking her little book. "As long as I am fed the requirements of the engagement will be met. I recorded no other conditions."

Binky slumped in resignation. "Fine. Lead on, Bentley."

The five of us raced through the club with Bentley in front. "We must use the rear entrance. The front is already sealed."

"Sealed by whom?" I panted.

"The Bureau of Collections, Sir. They are setting up a cordon around the club. Once it is complete you will be unable to leave for any reason until the debt is paid."

"Then, on the double, Bentley!"

We reached the back exit and Bentley scanned the street. Motioning to us to follow he moved swiftly to an enormous vehicle parked nearby. Its outlines seemed familiar and when Bentley pressed a button and a concealed door swung open, I recognized it at once. It was Cheeseworth's land yacht! We clambered aboard, the door closed behind us and we were safe. Alas, safe is a relative term. In the main compartment of the yacht, rising from her chair like the Kraken rising from the deep, her eyes piercing my very soul, was my indomitable Aunt Hypatia. There was no escape. I abandoned all hope and entered.

CHAPTER THREE

The Fellowship Assembles

My Aunt Hypatia has been called many things but almost all were uttered in the heat of anger. I get along with her better than most, chiefly because when we meet, I immediately roll onto my back and submit my vulnerable under-bits to her scaly claws. She can be a benevolent dragon when her fires are banked but one must always be on the lookout for flare-ups.

Behind my aunt was Uncle Hugo, who had been singed too many times to take any notice. He was feasting on canapés served by Cheeseworth's mechanical housekeeper Mrs. Cedar. Cheeseworth himself was feeding hay to his flock of pet sheep in a far corner of the room. My aunt glared at me over the rim of her teacup.

"Ah, nephew, this is a fine kettle of fish! Live free or die."

"Is it? Live free or die. To what do I owe the pleasure, Aunt?"

"Your uncle and I were just about to embark on a little motoring adventure…"

"Off to visit the seashore in Salisbury," my uncle shoved in glumly.

"Don't interrupt, Hugo. You are not nearly as interesting as you think you are. Sometimes I believe that even my low opinion of your charisma gives you too much credit. Where was I? Yes, we were going to view the remains of Salisbury before it is finally inundated by the rising seas, when Bentley told us that you must have the land yacht or be consumed by fire and flood."

"Isn't this Cheeseworth's vehicle?"

Cheeseworth stopped cramming hay into Compton's jaws and looked up. Compton took advantage of the lull to spit out a large ball of masticated vegetation and massage his aching jaws. Young Fred and his mother cowered in the corner, eyeing Cheeseworth fearfully.

"I lent them my yacht for their excursion, but if your need is gweater then consider it yours. Hello Euphonia... Cubby."

Cubby was staring about the luxurious interior with a smirk on his face. "The rich and their playthings," he muttered.

Euphonia gave him a smack and seated herself at the table. "Hush, Cubby. This is very cozy. I am quite content. Will we be dining soon?"

The door to the galley opened and Cook swept in carrying fresh canapés. She was Cook both by name and by occupation. I had acquired her services on an earlier adventure and her wizardry in the kitchen with fruits and vegetables put factory-made food to shame.

"Hello Cyril, love."

"Cook! What are you doing here?"

"Mr. Bentley said you needed me so I raided the larder and climbed aboard. Have a turnip cake."

She held out a tray and I popped a canapé into the old gaper. As usual it was scrumptious. My growling midsection reminded me that I had absconded from the club before the appearance of my cheesy eggs.

"Dinner will be ready in two shakes." She handed the tray to Mrs. Cedar and disappeared back into the galley.

"Hello, Mrs. Cedar."

"Hello Sir. It's very pleasant to see you again."

"How's that articulated joint? Bentley said it was giving you some trouble."

"Old age, Sir. Once you get past a hundred it's just patch, patch, patch."

"Well, you must take care of yourself. Cheeseworth House wouldn't be the same without you."

"Very kind of you to say so, I'm sure. I wonder if I might ask you if my wig is askew?"

"It is heeling a bit to windward."

"Thank you, Sir. There are no mirrors and I am continually brushing the ceiling with my head. The land yacht has a delightful economy of space but it is not designed for domestic servants of my dimensions."

She straightened her wig, bobbed a little curtsy and turned to offer a canapé to Cheeseworth.

I took a deep breath and looked around. "This is charming, I must say."

"But where are we going?" asked Binky. "We can't just sit here."

My aunt huffed. "No indeed. I did not set aside this time during the height of the season in order to go parking."

Bentley was watching the street through the window. "We should move expeditiously, Sir, and the more distant our destination the better."

He pulled some levers and the land yacht began to glide away from the curb. Out the back window I saw Null turning the corner with a troop of collection agents behind him. They were a rough looking bunch. Null Junior skipped beside her father swinging a baseball bat embedded with spikes. We had escaped in the nick of time!

I tapped on a wine glass to get everyone's attention. "Well, we're off. Can we drop you at your various homes?"

Cheeseworth clapped his hands gaily. "And miss the adventure? Boil me in oil if I wun away at the first hint of danger. We're coming with you."

"Yes, we shall simply incorporate your desperate flight to freedom into our plans for a pleasurable drive in the country," declared my aunt. "Nothing could be better. The prospect of being alone with your uncle was the only fly in the ointment. Now his company will be diluted by a large party and I shall barely be aware of him."

My uncle glared at her and produced a chorus of grunts and throat clearing. "Where are we off to then?"

I rubbed my hands together vigorously. "Where indeed? The world is our oyster, whatever an oyster is."

Binky bounced in his chair with his hand in the air. "I've always wanted to see the pyramids!"

"Afraid it's a land yacht, Old Ham. There's a considerable expanse of water between here and Egypt."

My aunt considered. "The sand dunes of Cambridge are said to be very like the trackless wastes of the Sinai Peninsula."

Suddenly I knew just where to go. There was an expedition I had been putting off for far too long.

"Bentley, set the autopilot for the Northern Wilderness."

"Could you be more specific, Sir?"

"No. We'll have to ask for more intelligence when we get closer. Just navigate us to the general vicinity."

Bentley worked the autopilot and the land yacht began to accelerate briskly.

My aunt looked at me suspiciously. "What is in the Northern Territories that draws you like a lodestar?"

I beamed at her triumphantly. "Chickens!"

My uncle glanced up at me sharply. "There have been no chickens since The Great Extinction. That is common knowledge."

My aunt nodded. "Usually when something contains the word 'common' I disregard it, but I see no reason to believe that this knowledge is specious."

I leaned in conspiratorially. "There have been rumours."

My aunt waved this away. "Oh... rumours. If you knew half the rumours circulating about you, you would not be so credulous about rumours."

"But if it were so, Aunt! Imagine the possibilities!"

"I am quite happy with chickeny nuggets. If people begin eating actual chickens, they will most certainly be extinct in no time."

"Not chickens... eggs!"

"What about them?"

"I remember eating one as a small child. The taste was indescribable! Imagine what Cook could do with them!"

As if conjured by the sound of her name, Cook popped out of the galley with a large, steaming vessel. "Vegetable tagine. Couscous with root vegetables and prunes. Eat up, everyone."

The party crowded around the table. My aunt glared at the delectable stew disdainfully.

"Hugo, we stocked the land yacht with provisions for our trip, did we not?"

"Indeed. There are boxes and boxes of vacuum-sealed meals."

"See if you can find me some sort of sandwich. Anything brown will do."

Cook put her hands on her hips and stared at my aunt icily. "Sandwiches!" she snorted. "Gammon and spinach!"

I shook my head sadly. "Really, Aunt, this tagine looks delicious. You are only punishing yourself."

"Your implication that I indulge in self-punishment is laughable. An overabundance of self-regard severs me irrevocably from the pleasures of masochism. I have, however, been accused of inciting the condition in others."

Cheeseworth waved a fork in the air. "I twied masochism once, but a mild tendency toward haemophilia made it impwactical."

Compton and his family were gazing longingly at the tagine. Cheeseworth fished out a carrot and flung it in their direction. There was a scramble and Compton got to it first. Breaking it into three small pieces he divided it among the family who sat, chewing slowly to make it last. Cook, who had observed this little melodrama, nipped into the kitchen and brought out three heaping bowls of tagine which she placed on the floor. Bleating gratefully, the flock tucked in.

My uncle had been rooting through a box and handed Aunt Hypatia a sandwich encased in plastic which she unwrapped and began to nibble at delicately. "Mmm... it could be beefy loaf or perhaps peanuty butter. Quite inoffensive."

"I believe mine is some sort of marine-based paste," observed Uncle Hugo, chewing lustily.

Cubby, who had not been a party to our conversation about destinations, was staring at the passing landscape with growing agitation. "I trust that we shall be returned to the club at the conclusion of this ill-omened meal."

I squirmed uncomfortably in my chair. "Ah... as to that... there may be some little delay before you can return to your duties as Club Marshall."

He leaped to his feet. "Stop this land yacht at once! Euphonia, we're leaving!"

His sister was unperturbed. "Oh, sit down, Cubby. This is delicious. I'm not leaving until I've had my pudding."

"You don't understand! Every second is taking us farther from home. Soon we will be unable to return without an extraordinary amount of bother."

Binky looked up hopefully. "What a shame. Must you go? I'm horribly disappointed but if Cubby feels it's best then I mustn't be selfish."

Bentley cleared his throat. "There are very comfortable sleeping compartments at the rear of the yacht. I anticipate that the situation should resolve itself in a matter of days and you will be returned safely to your place of origin."

Cubby stared about wildly. "Kidnapped again! I was a fool to trust myself to another of your mad schemes, Chippington-Smythe."

He was referring, of course, to an earlier adventure in which Cubby and Euphonia had been unwilling passengers on my dirigible during a flight to New York City.

I tried to soothe him. "Now, Cubby, it turned out fine the last time, didn't it? We got you home in one piece. Why not enjoy this beautiful tagine?"

He crossed his arms and looked at me stonily.

"No, thank you. Just a glass of water, please."

"You're not going to starve yourself!"

"Eating the food of my abductors would be a tacit acceptance of the situation, therefore I must refuse."

I sighed. "Suit yourself. More for the rest of us."

Euphonia had happily refilled her plate and was shoveling it in. "Well, I'm very happy. I feel that a young person like myself should have as many adventures as possible. That way I shall have something exciting to read about when I am old. Besides, Mr. Wickford-Davies would be heartbroken. He is in love with me."

Binky gave a start. "What? Why do you say that?"

"I read all about it earlier." Euphonia was leafing through her little book. "Here we are... page sixteen... yes, you are desperately in love with me, Mr. Wickford-Davies."

"Is that what it says?"

"It is there in black and white. You must have made quite an impression."

"Well, but... you can't believe everything you read you know."

"I am scrupulous in my entries. I must be. This little book takes the place of my memory and therefore I must be able to trust it absolutely. You haven't yet proposed to me, have you? No, I would certainly have made a note of it. When you do, make certain that I have written it down."

Binky had grown pale. "Look here, Euphonia, you're a crackerjack young lady, but I'm known as rather a playboy, you know. You don't want to get mixed up with someone like me."

I stifled a giggle and Binky shot me a venomous look. Cubby was watching everything through narrowed eyes.

"Be very careful, Wickford-Davies... and you too, Chippington-Smythe. If I thought either of you was toying with my sister, I would have no alternative but to call you out."

"Never in life," I exclaimed. "I have the highest regard for Euphonia and I'm sure that Binky here feels the same way."

Euphonia was scribbling in her little book. She looked up happily. "It is very gratifying to be fought over by two such eligible young men."

I was aghast. "Fought over? No, there's been a little misunderstanding."

Cubby fingered his cutlery and picked up his knife. I hurriedly retreated. "Well, all this talk of romance has given me an appetite. Pass that couscous, won't you?"

The company settled in and tried to do justice to Cook's tagine. At last, I leaned back and loosened my belt a notch.

"That hit the spot. I feel almost human again."

Cook bustled in with a large bowl. "Tapioca pudding with apricots. Enjoy."

I turned around in my seat and beckoned her over.

"I say, Cook. Could I ask you about something?"

"Of course, Love."

"Have you ever cooked... eggs?"

A dreamy look appeared on her face. "I remember when you could still get your hands on an egg or two. Magical things! There are a thousand dishes you can make with eggs: meringues; souffles; frittatas. What I wouldn't give for a dozen eggs!"

I grinned at her. "I'm happy to hear it! We're on our way to get you some."

"Are we? I thought chickens were no more."

"Rumour has it that a small flock escaped The Great Extinction and has been quietly propagating in the Northern Wilderness."

She thought this over with her hands on her hips. "Well, you get me the eggs and I'll know what to do with them."

My uncle looked at me keenly. "Is it your intention to begin commercial farming of chickens? Such a venture would be quite lucrative."

"I mean to begin with eggs."

"But surely chickens must come first."

"That's what Bentley says, but eggs hatch into chickens and are easier to carry. Also, you don't have to feed them. There are countless advantages."

Cheeseworth was eyeing his flock of sheep thoughtfully. "Don't have to feed them, eh? They sound like ideal pets." Compton and his family began to baa nervously.

"I think a pet egg would be boring," mused Binky. "It can't come when you call or snuggle in bed on a rainy day."

"Also, it would eventually hatch into a chicken and then you're right back where you started," observed my uncle.

My interest in the chicken/egg controversy was beginning to flag. The sky was growing dark outside the land yacht. We had left the last signs of civilization behind some time ago and were passing through a rather arid-looking landscape. Dinner having concluded, the party divided itself into small conclaves and commenced chatting.

Binky pulled me aside into a quiet alcove. He looked around to make sure we couldn't be overheard.

"Listen, Cyril, I've had a brainstorm about Euphonia."

"Have you?" I was naturally suspicious. Binky's brainstorms usually involved wearing fake moustaches and speaking in foreign accents or scaling dizzying heights with a grappling hook and line.

"She only remembers what she's written in that little book of hers, correct?"

"So it would seem."

"Then all we've got to do is tear out the parts about us being in love with her and it will be as if it never happened."

The logic of this rather stunned me. I wracked my brain looking for the fatal flaw that must be there, but came up empty. "By Jove, I don't suppose even Bentley could come up with something better! Now, how are we going to get it away from her? She wears it twenty-four hours a day."

Binky pondered. "What if we spilled hot soup in her lap? She'd have to change."

"But she could change her skirt without removing the notebook from around her neck."

"Could we set it on fire?"

"Not without burning Euphonia up as well."

"Stinging ants?"

"I don't have any, do you?"

"Not at the moment. Damn! This is harder than I imagined."

Whenever my brain begins to overheat, it sends out a desperate call for help. "I know! Let's ask Bentley!"

"Rather! Come on."

We thundered to the back of the land yacht where Bentley was unpacking luggage. In a few well-chosen phrases we conveyed the meat of the situation. His gears ground away merrily.

"As I understand it, the salient point is how to separate Ms. Gumboot from the notebook that she keeps on her person at all times without causing her bodily harm."

"That's it exactly. What's the plan?"

He stared inward for a moment, then chugged back into animation. "I have no concrete suggestion at this time. I shall watch and wait for an opportunity. We must seize our chance when it comes."

"Carpe notebook, as it were."

"Yes, Sir."

Binky looked crestfallen. "What if she never takes it off?"

"We must cross that bridge when we come to it." Bentley returned to his unpacking and we rejoined the company. My uncle was regaling everyone with the latest news on the Delivery Persons' Race scandal.

"No witnesses, no clues. It seems that whoever engineered this caper will escape without retribution."

My aunt sniffed. "You can be sure that the act was committed by anarchists. They will stop at nothing in their attempts to gnaw away at the supports of society—like the bygone beavers and their rapacious ilk."

"We were just talking about this at the club," I observed as I plopped myself into an overstuffed chair. "Ford was asking who benefited from Ernie getting nobbled?"

My uncle scowled. "That's the devil of it. The stewards have gone through the wagers and there were no bets on the actual winner. It seems that no one wound up better off."

"Who was the winner, by the way?" I inquired.

"Who indeed?" My aunt looked thoughtful. "He had a foreign name, which conjured up images of vineyards and ruined palazzos. What was it? Manuel? Marco?"

Bentley glided forward. "Mario Grubenspieler, Ma'am."

"Was it? He was a hirsute fellow with a luxurious moustache. I wonder if he's any relation to the Grubenspielers of Whyte on Rhyce?"

Cubby was staring out of the window but he turned with a snort.

"You can hardly suspect Mr. Grubenspieler. He ran a clean race in full view of the spectators and was declared the winner. It would be a terrible injustice if his accomplishments were to be tarnished by unfounded accusations."

"No one is accusing anyone, but those wheels didn't jump off of Ernie's cart by themselves," I noted. "If there's any injustice it's that Ernie should have been the winner."

"And I should be rolling in obscene profits instead of fleeing the hounds of the collection agency," sniffed Binky.

"The crux of the matter is who fixed the race," I said thoughtfully. "If there is any connection to this Grubenspieler chap then the mystery is solved."

Cubby rose from his seat. "I know Mr. Grubenspieler. He has delivered for years to many distinguished members of the club. He is above suspicion."

"Then what's your idea?"

"I believe the race results will stand and that Mr. Wickford-Davies will find himself in debtor's prison within the week."

"You'd love that, wouldn't you," exclaimed Binky, whose eyes were turning pink. "You've always resented me because I'm popular and you're not!"

I stepped between them. "Steady now, we're not sixteen."

Cubby would not be silenced. "I resent you, Wickford-Davies, because you take your position in society for granted. What do you have to recommend you but an accident of birth? There are others with ability and accomplishments who are forever barred from the exalted waters in which you swim, yet you display no trace of humility or gratitude. You sail through life and the icebergs that sink the less fortunate are simply swept out of your path. Do you deny it?"

Binky worked his mouth a few times, then blushed and looked down at his feet. "I do not deny it, but what would you have me do about it? What would you do if you were me?"

This seemed to rather stump Cubby. He sputtered a bit then muttered some disjointed phrases about "show some humility" and "give others a leg up." Finally, they both fell silent and the company sank into an awkward silence. My aunt finally rose to her feet.

"This awkward caesura signals that it is time to retire. Lifting the conversation from the floor, where it lies gasping like a defeated prizefighter would require the strength of Atlas. Could I accomplish it? Of course, but it would be a shocking waste of my resources. Hugo, come!"

She sailed down the aisle to her sleeping compartment with Uncle Hugo in her wake. The rest of the company followed her example and in no time, we were all snug in our little sleeping compartments. The land yacht hummed down the asphalt and the vibration of its wheels was soporific. I sank into the arms of Morpheus and dreamed of eggs.

Chapter Four

We Locate Our Quarry

I was awakened by the rosy-fingered dawn and after a quick wash and brush-up, I pounded over to the breakfast table where Cook had laid out her customary morning buffet. Pancakes, muffins, porridge, potatoes—it was a feast that would have satisfied Epicurus. I tucked in and was soon joined by the various members of the company, who filled their plates and sat chewing in silence. Compton and his family crept out from under the sofa and were given bowls of porridge by Cook. They reached for spoons but a loud "Harrumph" from Cheeseworth caused them to flinch and they ended by plopping their faces into their bowls and making loud lapping noises.

At last, the platters were cleared and we sat sipping tea and observing the scenery. The arid plains of York had given way to the dense forests of the North. Bentley distilled himself out of the ether at my elbow.

"We must choose a more specific destination soon, Sir."

"Very good. Stop by the next inhabitant you see and we'll gather intelligence."

It wasn't long before the land yacht slowed to a halt. I leaned out of the window and found a tall, muscular fellow with a long staff staring back at me.

"Good morning, my good man!"

"What's good about it?"

I pulled my head back inside and looked around. "He wants to know what's good about it?"

My aunt considered. "The humidity is unusually low, but he may prefer high humidity so that is a risky approach."

Cheeseworth was lying on the sofa but he lifted his head to observe, "I had a nocturnal emission."

"I don't think that would necessarily cheer him up, but thank you."

Binky raised his hand. "Why not offer him a muffin? That would improve anyone's morning."

"I think you're on to something there. Hand me one of the blueberry variety."

I leaned back out of the window and passed the gentleman a muffin. "Does that sufficiently deal with the quality-of-morning issue?"

He took a nibble. His eyes lit up and he tucked in. The muffin was gone in two bites. "Aye, it's a good morning after all." He turned and began to walk away.

"I say," I called after him. "I did have a question."

He turned back. "Why didn't ye say so?"

"Have you heard the rumours that there are chickens living in the Northern Wilderness?"

"Oh, aye, everyone knows that."

I pulled my head in. "He says the rumours are true. He says everyone knows about it."

"Boastful fellow," huffed my aunt. "I cannot abide people who claim to know things of which I am unaware. These are merely facts, which can be learned by any common lag-about. What is more difficult to cultivate is an air of knowing everything. It has taken me a lifetime to acquire it whereas all this bumpkin can do is to regurgitate facts will you nill you like a geek in a sideshow."

I poked my head back out the window to find our new acquaintance wistfully licking the paper that had encased his muffin. I hastily handed him another. "Could you direct us to the locality where these chickens have been observed?"

"Oh, aye, stay on the motorway and you'll come to a gravel road that goes off to the right. Follow that for a few miles and you'll find someone who can give you more directions."

"Thank you very much, my good fellow. I am in your debt."

He looked at me shrewdly. "I wouldn't say nae to a few more of those muffins."

I grabbed the basket and handed it to him. He pulled a forelock and hurried off with his treasure cradled in his arms

"Take the next road to the right, Bentley," I called out.

"Very good, Sir."

We soon reached the turn and Bentley swung the land yacht off the main road. As we crawled down the poorly maintained gravel lane, we began to see signs posted on the trees. "Up With Chickens!" was popular, as was "Chickens Before Eggs."

Binky sounded them out laboriously. "I say, it looks like we're in the right place."

As the signs grew more numerous, they were joined by crude representations of chickens made from sticks and moss. Some were tiny, some as big as cars. Finally, we saw one of the inhabitants of the area. He was hammering another sign onto a tree. It read, "Don't be a dumb cluck—choose chickens!"

We pulled over to see if we could gather some navigational assistance. The citizen in question wore a vest of feathers and had his hair drawn up into a kind of coxcomb. I opened a window and waved at him.

"Good morning, my good fellow!"

He looked at me suspiciously. "Chickens before eggs," he exclaimed.

"Indeed. I wonder if I could ask you for some information?"

He squinted at me truculently. "Chickens before eggs," he repeated.

Bentley appeared at my elbow. "I believe it is a motto in the vein of 'Live Free or Die,' Sir. He expects a reply."

"Ah, got it." I leaned out the window. "Chickens before eggs!"

This seemed to reassure him. He sidled a little closer. "Where are ye from?"

"We're from the city. We've come up here following rumours of chickens."

"Oh aye? What about them?"

"Have you seen any?"

"That depends. Which side are ye on?"

"Side?"

"Chicken or egg? If you're an Eggnostic I'll have naught to do with ye."

I pulled my head in to confer. "I must say, I've always been more partial to eggs. Does that make me an Eggnostic?"

"But if you tell him that he won't talk to us," observed Binky.

Bentley stepped to the window. "I shall speak to him, Sir." He leaned out. "I am firmly on the side of chickens, Sir. I believe they are superior to eggs in every way. Does that satisfy you?"

The man rubbed his chin and nodded. "Aye, that'll do. Keep down this road for another mile or two and you'll find the town. They can tell you all you want to know about chickens."

"Thank you, my good man. Chickens before eggs."

Bentley pulled his head back in and took the wheel. We rolled on down the road and in a short while we crested a ridge and observed a small hamlet. In the center of it was a wooden chicken the size of a house! The local citizenry plodded here and there in typical fashion. The general aesthetic was feathery. There were feathered vests and elaborate feathered headgear. There was also a distinct odour that was at once sharp and fetid. We embarked from the land yacht and stood staring up at the enormous chicken effigy before us.

A voice spoke in my ear. "Why, It's Mr. Chippington-Smythe, isn't it?"

I whirled around to find a round little man with a familiar smiling face. "Ahmed Ben Fitzwilliam?"

"Good morning, Sir. Yes, that is my name, but I am more commonly known in these parts as The High Chickian."

"Everyone, this is Mr. Fitzwilliam, the Club Hatter of Twits."

There was a general gabble of salutations but Fitzwilliam blushed and looked away.

"Thank you all, but alas, hats went out of fashion last season and my profession ceased to exist."

"Bad luck. I say, what are you doing here?"

"It was fate, Sir. The capricious banning of headgear by the arbiters of taste left me marooned. I tried designing hats for the masses, but I was unable to lower my aesthetic to a price point that made it feasible. At last, I was evicted from my home and forced to live the life of a wandering peddler. I drifted North, trading hats that I crafted from bark and leaves for food, until I stumbled upon this little village. I saw the potential at once. The citizens here had never heard of fashion! They went about their lives, farming and trading with the village across the river, but with no style, no panache! I have introduced elegance and sophistication, and elevated what was once dull commerce into a celebration of patriotism and pageantry!"

"This is a stroke of luck, running into you. What do you know about chickens?"

He bowed his head solemnly. "I think I can say with some modesty that I know as much about chickens as any man living."

My aunt gave a sniff. "These frenzies of specialized knowledge are known to cause psychosis. A kind of vague general knowledge about a variety of topics is much healthier. Whenever I learn too much about a subject, I immediately banish it from my conversation and refuse to learn any more about it."

I left a respectful pause and turned back to Fitzwilliam. "Look here, we've come a long way following rumours of chickens living in the wild. Are these stories true?"

"Alas, there are no chickens in the wild, Sir."

My heart plummeted. "So, they're extinct after all?"

"I did not say that. There are no chickens in the wild because they are all here."

I looked around. "Where?"

"Follow me. I will show you."

Fitzwilliam went striding off and we were forced to move briskly to keep up. Compton and his family brought up the rear, with Cheeseworth swinging his shepherd's crook pretty liberally. Fitzwilliam led us to an enormously long structure that fronted on the town square. It was from this edifice that the richly pungent odour emanated. A couple of beefy guards stood by the entrance but they stepped aside when they saw Fitzwilliam.

"Behold the Temple Pullum. Here these noble birds are protected and nurtured. Enter!"

We pushed through the wooden doorway and were engulfed in pandemonium. Chickens were everywhere! Chickens of every age and description squawked and strutted. There was barely room for them to move about and the air was so thick with feathers and dust that it was more a solid than a gas. I gagged and pulled my shirt up to cover my face.

My aunt turned at once and headed for the exit. "This is intolerable! If this is what nature is like then I choose artifice. I shall place myself upwind of this acidic aroma until you have satisfied your morbid curiosity."

She swept out, followed by most of our party. Only Binky and Uncle Hugo stood the course. I watched the workers inside the temple as they carefully shuffled their feet to avoid trampling on the sea of chickens around them. Occasionally they would stoop and recover a newly laid egg which they carefully set in baskets attached to their midsections. The chickens themselves looked miserable. They shoved and pecked at each other but there was no way for them to move about freely.

Uncle Hugo had a strange gleam in his eye. "They might as well be made of gold! The value of this flock is incalculable!"

I peered at the birds struggling to squeeze past my shoes. "I say, do they enjoy living like this?"

Fitzwilliam shrugged. "Who can guess the thoughts of such noble creatures? I assume that if they wished for anything more, they would inform us."

"It just seems rather crowded, you know."

"Yes, we receive more chicks each evening and chickens live five to ten years, so the increase is exponential."

Binky was practically drooling. "Have you ever thought of reducing their numbers by roasting a few of them?"

A nearby guard spun around to stare at Binky. Fitzwilliam grew pale. He shooed us out of the temple. We carefully shuffled our feet as the workers did to avoid treading on the tiny chicken claws around us.

As soon as we cleared the door, Fitzwilliam spoke to us urgently in a low voice. "Please do not say such things aloud, my friends. Nothing about..." he nervously pulled at his collar, "eating chickens! I know you're joking, of course, but the citizenry might get the wrong idea."

I looked at him in surprise. "You mean you don't eat them? Why on earth not?"

"Legend has it that they're delicious," said Binky.

He gasped and made shushing motions whilst darting looks at the nearby guards. "They are sacred! You can't eat sacred birds! It would set a terrible precedent. Once you start down that road what other sacred things might find their way onto the menu?"

I suddenly felt something pulling at the cuff of my trousers. I looked down to find a plump little red hen pecking at my shoelace. Fitzwilliam goggled.

"You have been favoured! This is a great honour."

The guards at the doorway looked mortified at having let one of their charges slip through security. They started forward but Fitzwilliam raised a hand.

"Leave her be. If she has chosen to vouchsafe her favours, then we must not interfere."

"That's all well and good," I observed, "But how do I stop her from trying to eat my shoelace?"

"You don't. She must be allowed to express herself freely. I'm afraid you must acquiesce to whatever she chooses to bestow on you."

"Hello! She's bestowed herself on my shoe!"

"Do not wipe it off! She has blessed your shoe. The blessing must remain. So it is written."

I gently stepped away from the little hen but she happily followed my shoelace as it dragged in the dust. I tried zigging and zagging a bit but she kept up with me easily.

Fitzwilliam scratched his chin. "It seems you have gained a companion."

"It does, rather. Perhaps I should give her a name. What about Cackles?"

As if in response, the little bird emitted a loud squawk.

"She seems to like it. All right, Cackles, then."

My Uncle Hugo had been observing all this with a deep frown. He turned to Fitzwilliam. "Are we to understand that you worship chickens? How on earth did such a thing transpire?"

Fitzwilliam held up a palm. "Worship is perhaps too strong a word. We do not consider chickens to be supernatural. We honour them because they have survived when so many species did not. We respect them as symbols of a golden age that exists only in the memories of the most aged among us. We appreciate them for their contributions to our well-being."

"But you don't eat them," my uncle observed, "So what is their contribution?"

Fitzwilliam bowed his head. "Glory to chickens," he intoned. "Noble birds! Destroyers of ticks and grubs. Givers of fertile droppings that nourish our crops and pretty feathers to adorn our bodies withal. All hail!"

We were interrupted by the missing members of our little band as they rejoined the party. Cackles inspected each of them closely and when she reached Cheeseworth's flock she gave a squawk. She turned her head sideways to stare at them then looked back at me questioningly.

"They're sheep," I said, in answer to her unspoken query. "Nice sheepies. Give them a peck, girl."

She looked at me archly, turned her back on Compton and his family and scratched some dirt in their direction.

"I say," observed Cheeseworth, "Something's going on down by the bwidge."

Fitzwilliam clapped his hands with excitement. "It is six o'clock. Now you'll see something! Each evening we collect the eggs that have been laid during the day and exchange them for the chicks that have hatched across the river. Thus both communities are purified."

"Purified of what?" I enquired.

"No time to explain. Follow me!"

CHAPTER FIVE

A Bit of Pageantry

We hurried down to the river and found places among the crowd of onlookers. A long elaborate carpet had been rolled across the bridge and there were parties of celebrants gathered on either side of the river. On our side, the participants were dressed in feathers with enormous plumed headpieces.

"We call ourselves the 'Chickians' and the other village has adopted the moniker 'Eggnostics.' I must take my place. Come and stand behind me." Fitzwilliam stepped up on a slightly elevated piece of bluff and held up his hand as a signal. As the Chickians stepped onto the bridge the other contingent did the same.

The approaching Eggnostics were dressed in ceremonial white. Their heads were encased in shiny white egg-shaped helmets. The leaders of the procession held long staves shaped rather like forks. Behind them strode a phalanx of smart-stepping citizens carrying baskets full of loudly cheeping, buttery yellow chicks.

Fitzwilliam gestured and the Chickian contingent started forward. The leader carried a spear in the form of a giant butter knife. His followers carried baskets filled with mounds of eggs.

The two sides met in the middle of the bridge and stamped to a halt. The leaders stepped forward and faced each other. Fitzwilliam nudged me in the ribs. "This is the ceremonial exchange. We do it each evening just before sunset. Observe!"

The Chickian representative began to strut in a most eccentric manner. He scratched at the ground and shot his head forward and back like a jackhammer, making his feathered headpiece flutter. This was accompanied by a loud clucking sound. After a moment the lead Eggnostic squatted down. He held his knees to form a roundish sort of lump and began to slowly roll in a circle. At last, the two groups of dancers faced each other. The Chickians began a cacophony of squawks and clucks. The Eggnostics rolled forward and back in a threatening fashion. Their movements gained in intensity until at some invisible signal everyone froze.

"Thrilling, is it not?" chortled Fitzwilliam. "I designed the headgear of course. I still dabble from time to time."

Binky's eyes were like moons. "What happens now?"

"Now comes the ceremonial exchange of chicks and eggs. Observe."

The basket-carriers stepped forward. Walking with a kind of step-slide choreography, they met in the center of the bridge. They handed the baskets full of chicks and eggs to each other with solemn faces and backed away. Now the two opposing factions turned and casually walked away from each other.

"Finita!" Fitzwilliam clapped his hands. "We have been cleansed of the foul eggs that infested us."

Binky looked confused. "What's wrong with the eggs? Had they gone bad?"

Fitzwilliam frowned. "Eggs do not *go* bad. They are bad by their very nature. They cannot change their fundamental wickedness by any means. No amount of good works can alter the balance. The only alternative is to expel them before their evil infects us all."

My aunt nodded. "Then they are like Whigs. They cannot be rehabilitated. They must be eliminated."

Cheeseworth looked thoughtful. "I believe in the power of wehabilitation. If I did not, I would still be labouring at that pwison farm on Tortuga. Hard labour made a man of me and I believe that these eggs would benefit fwom a similar course of discipline."

My Uncle snorted. "This is the false promise of the penal system. Forcing eggs to work in the hot sun would only make them more hard-boiled."

I was growing a little lightheaded. "Look here, we *are* talking about eggs, aren't we?"

"Yes— wicked, deceitful eggs," Fitzwilliam confirmed.

"How can they be deceitful? They can't speak."

"Can't or won't? There is a wise old saying that silence is acceptance—but acceptance of what? They refuse to say. Their reticence is infuriating! Until they categorically deny that they are on the side of evil then we must assume the worst. That is why they cannot remain among us. If we allow their numbers to grow, they may someday overpower us by sheer force of numbers and alter our way of life to disastrous effect."

I peered at him closely. "Is this philosophy something you came up with?"

"I picked up a great deal of it from conversations I overheard at the club, Sir. There is a surprising amount of vitriol under the civilized veneer."

My uncle nodded. "I thought it sounded familiar."

My eye was suddenly drawn to a pair of robed figures standing at the top of a bluff on the opposite shore. They wore egg-shaped hats that towered over them. There was something strangely familiar about the two of them. With a start, I realized that they were my old TV— Smith and Jones! Bentley had chained the entertainers to a radiator when we were called away on an emergency some time ago. Hunger and thirst had driven the entertainers to file through the fetters that confined them to my parlour and make good their escape some months ago. What odd current had washed them up on this curious shore?

"Excuse me everyone, I have to nip across the river for a moment. I've just seen some people I believe I know."

Ahmed Ben Fitzwilliam nodded. "I shall chaperone your friends around the village. There are many more chicken-centric sights to see."

Cheeseworth tapped his sheep on their backs with his crook thoughtfully. "I wonder what sort of relationship existed between sheep and chickens in times of old. Were they natural enemies, do you suppose? Did sheep feast on the slaughtered wemains of these birds, or were they fwiends?"

Compton looked up nervously. "I've got nothing against chickens personally, Sir. I'd rather not feast on any slaughtered remains, if you don't mind."

"Me? What has is to do with me? It is nature—'red in tooth and claw.' You will follow your natural instincts, whatever they may be."

"Then if it's all the same to you, Sir, we'd like to be friends."

Cheeseworth sighed. "Vewy well. Less dramatic, perhaps, but twue to your natures."

As I stepped out toward the bridge, Cackles happily waddled after me. Fitzwilliam hopped in front of us.

"I'm afraid Cackles must stay on this side of the river, Sir. The other villagers do not allow chickens amongst them."

"Well tell *her* that. Whither I go, it seems, she goes."

The former hatter leaned down and gently picked the little hen up. He winced as she pecked at him to register her objections, but he held fast.

"I shall watch over her until your return."

"Good-oh. Thanks awfully."

I headed for the bridge, which was empty of celebrants now, and trotted across to the opposite shore. Two Eggnostics, still in their robes, barred my way.

"Eggs before chickens," they grunted at me.

"Oh, indeed. Eggs before chickens," I answered. They inspected me suspiciously for a few moments then stepped aside.

I climbed up the hill toward the pair of white-clad entertainers. As I drew near, Smith suddenly spotted me. His eyes started and his mouth fell open. He seized his partner's hand and dragged her down the street, whispering urgently in her ear. She glanced back at me fearfully and the two of them broke into a dead run. They made a sudden turn and leaped into a compost heap by the side of the road. I stared at the quaking heap of decomposing vegetation curiously. Strolling up to it I poked at it with a toe.

"Hallo. Everything all right in there?"

Smith's voice issued from under a cabbage leaf. "Oh yes, Sir. Thank you for inquiring. Nothing to see here. Enjoy your stroll."

One of Jones's eyes peeped out from behind a mound of carrot peelings. "What's that happening down the street? I think they've struck gold, Sir! Better run! Don't worry about us."

I peered down the street but the only movement was a small child hitting a rock with a stick. I addressed the pile again. "I say, aren't you my old TV, Smith and Jones?"

There was a pause and the heap vibrated nervously.

"Never heard of them. We're Wallace and Davis."

"Never worked in show business, Sir. Uncertain profession. Infrequent meals. Chain you to a radiator if you give them half a chance."

I gave the mound a poke. "I knew it was you! What are you doing here? Why are you dressed in those outfits?"

Jones's head slowly emerged from the vegetation. "You're not angry with us, Sir?"

"Angry? No, why should I be?"

"Well, we escaped, after all. Technically we're still your TV."

Now Smith made his appearance. "It's not like us to scarper on an engagement. That Mr. Bentley made life impossible. We have often thought back on our actions with regret, Sir."

"Not at all. You were quite right to throw off your shackles. Don't give it a second thought."

"Do you mean it, Sir?"

"I do. Consider yourself released from my employment."

Their eyes grew misty. Jones blew her nose loudly into her sleeve. "You're too good by half, Sir. We don't deserve it."

"But what are you doing here?"

Smith brushed the leaves and twigs from his robe. "We thought it best to put some distance between us and any possible retribution for our flight. We were buskers in our younger days, so we donned the buttons again and busked our way north. When we reached this town, they were just beginning to develop the pageant that takes place each evening with the village across the river. You've met Mr. Fitzwilliam?"

"I have."

"He's very good with the costumes, but he had no theatrical training. We pitched in with some choreography and wrote a little dialogue to go with it and in return they made us 'The High Eggnostics.'"

Jones removed her egg-shaped hat and held it out for my inspection. "Look at that workmanship! It matches anything we wore in the Brighton Beach Follies. We get room and board plus pocket money."

"We put on a little show every Friday night to keep in practice. It's a steady gig and at our age we really can't ask for more." Smith wiped a tiny tear from the corner of his eye.

I was struck by a sudden thought. "Your village has rather a monopoly on eggs, what?"

"Oh yes. The Chickians won't have anything to do with them so we've pretty much cornered the market on eggs."

"Well, look here, I'm rather interested in acquiring some."

They grew silent and stared at me. Finally, Smith cleared his throat. "I'm afraid that's impossible, Sir."

"Why is that?"

Jones looked down at her toes. "They're sacred, you know. No one's allowed to touch them except the Brooders, and even they can't put their hands on them."

"Who are the Brooders?"

"They sit on the eggs to hatch them. They can only touch them with the... uh... appropriate parts of their anatomy."

This was all a little much for me. "You don't mean to say... that is... doesn't anyone eat any of the eggs?"

They looked at me with horror.

"Don't let any of the citizens hear you say that," whispered Smith hoarsely. "There's no telling what might happen."

"But I came all this way because it has been the dream of my life to once again taste the ambrosia of a perfectly fried egg."

Smith and Jones clapped their hands to their ears and rocked back and forth.

"Please don't say such things, Sir!"

"I'm afraid I'm going to be sick."

This was a disappointment and no mistake. "It seems I have traveled all this way in vain."

"You have, Sir, if your intention was to masticate a sacred egg."

"But what's sacred about them?"

Jones crossed her arms over her chest and assumed a beatific look. "Oh, Egg... spark of life... repository of mysteries... your perfect roundness has no beginning nor no end. In your eloquent silence we find peace. All hail the egg—which definitely came before the chicken."

"You know, across the river they think it's chickens that are sacred," I noted.

Smith waved this off with a snort. "Have you smelled them, Sir? I think that should settle the debate."

"It seems there are irreconcilable differences between the two villages."

"I'm afraid so. We feel a little guilty about that. They used to be very friendly, but the theatricality of the evening ritual required conflict—every good dramatist knows that, and so it had to be done."

"There hasn't been any violence, has there?"

"Not yet, Sir, but it's only a matter of time," sighed Jones. "Of course, the violence will only increase our village's devotion to eggs, which will strengthen our position accordingly."

"We ought to be in line for a healthy raise, what with the combat pay and all."

"Oh, but look here, that's beastly."

Smith grew defensive. "It's human nature, Sir. We can't change that."

"If we tried, they'd only turn on us," Jones agreed. "What's the good of that?"

"And if they drive us out, someone worse would certainly take our place."

"Yes, but... well... I can't put it into words but it just feels rather rotten."

Smith looked at me coldly. "We're sorry you feel that way, Sir. I'm afraid we must be going. It's time for the ceremonial turning of the eggs."

"Lovely to see you again, Sir. Please be careful what you say until you're safely back on the other side of the river."

There was a lot to consider as I trudged back across the bridge. I had observed battles between opposing factions before. I myself had suffered a vicious "pantsing" at the club when my merry band of "Shakens" had encountered a superior force of "Stirreds," but this conflict looked as if it was headed for bloodshed. Clearly it would be best to acquire the eggs we sought and scamper away while our hides were still intact. Alas, there was going to be a distinct lack of "scampering" in my future, for I was about to stick my foot in it up to the ankle.

Chapter Six

A Sudden Detour

Bridges in fiction are notorious for sheltering trolls beneath their spans, but the only semi-human lingering in the shade as I stepped onto the bank was Binky. He rushed over, scanned the area to confirm that we were alone, and pulled me into the shadows.

"Look here," he began, "All this hither and yonning you're doing is causing you to lose sight of our main objective."

"Keeping you out of debtor's prison?"

He stopped dead. "I'd forgotten about that."

"You can bet Null and his daughter haven't forgotten."

"All right, you've lost sight of our secondary objective."

"And what might that be?"

"Getting that notebook away from Euphonia!"

"I thought Bentley was taking care of that."

"He's had plenty of time and nothing is happening."

"Well, what do you want me to do about it?"

He drew close enough for me to smell his cologne... "Insouciance"... fruity, with overtones of musk. A sly smile played about the corners of his lips. "I've got a plan."

I recoiled. "That phrase always gives me the shivers."

"It's a sure thing."

"That one's even worse."

"Examine this bridge."

I gave it the once-over. "What about it?"

"It's only a foot or so above the water. There's no possibility of injury."

"Injury to whom?"

"To Euphonia, when you push her in."

"Why the blazes would I do that?"

"Because she'll have to change her clothes and that will give Bentley the perfect opportunity to nip her notebook and tear out those pages."

I digested this nugget. "But why am *I* doing the pushing? It's your plan."

"I'm the first one Cubby would suspect. No one would expect such a devious plot from you. You're too straightforward."

I shook my head firmly. "Well, I won't do it. You'll have to come up with something else."

"There is nothing else! This is our last chance. Don't forget— you're listed in that little book as one of her swains too."

I groaned inwardly.

"And stop groaning."

"Sorry, I thought I'd groaned *inwardly*."

"You see that I'm right. It's got to be done."

"But how am I to get her onto the bridge in the first place?"

"It doesn't matter. Whatever stratagem you employ will be forgotten in no time. That's the most charming thing about Euphonia. Just tell her you've got to speak to her, walk her out on the bridge and give her a good shove."

"And what will you be doing?"

"Preparing an alibi."

"I've got a better idea. While I'm pushing Euphonia into the drink, you sneak in and slide an egg or two out from under some of those chickens."

He frowned and shook his head. "You don't want me handling delicate things. I get the shakes and my fingers go all numb. I'm like a bull in a chowder shop."

"A what?"

"You know, one of those ancient beasts with horns."

"But what's it doing in a chowder shop?"

"It's a saying, you know. Apparently they couldn't hold those little bowls of chowder with their hooves, so they were always dropping them and smashing them to smithereens. Chowder everywhere. The chowder merchants were in despair."

"No eggs, no pushing. That is my condition. Take it or leave it."

"What if I get pecked?"

"I'm counting on it."

He frowned and produced some discontented noises. "Oh... fine! How many do you want?"

"Three or four should be sufficient."

"I'd better nab five or six to account for mishaps. Good luck."

Binky slunk away, dodging from shadow to shadow and looking extremely suspicious. I heard a squawk from the direction of my ankles. Cackles had apparently escaped from her keeper and was once again happily attempting to swallow my shoelace.

"Hallo, Old Girl. I hope your day is going better than mine."

I was ruminating on how to lure Euphonia onto the bridge when the party in question strolled out from behind a bush and headed straight for me.

As she drew near, Cackles eyed her suspiciously. She waddled forward and pecked at the ground truculently. Euphonia bent down and gave her little head a pat, which seemed to win her over. She headed back to my ankle and Euphonia followed her.

"Hello. We've met, haven't we?"

"Yes. I'm Cyril. Page sixteen, I believe."

She riffled through her notebook, read an entry and looked up with a smile. "Oh yes, you are one of the gentlemen who are in love with me."

I did my best to conceal the shudder that ran down my spine. "Well, *love* is a slippery thing, isn't it? You think you know just where it is but when you reach for it, it's nipped out the back or fallen down a well."

She smiled warmly. "You speak as one who is intimately acquainted with the condition."

Suddenly there was nothing I wanted more dearly than to shove Euphonia into some cold water. "Let's set that aside for a moment. There's something I want to show you. It's down there, in the river." I pointed into the water.

Euphonia joined me and stared down into the depths. "I don't see anything."

"Just keep looking," I urged her. I backed up a few steps to get a running start. I began to sprint toward her and that's when Cubby came around a corner and stared straight at me. Altering course at the last second, I managed to avoid Euphonia and plunged headlong off the bridge and into the icy water. I emerged, sputtering, and dog-paddled to the bank. Euphonia trotted over and stared at me. Cackles squawked hysterically and paced back and forth by the river's edge flapping her wings.

Cubby had drawn near and watched me climb out of the river suspiciously. "What are you up to, Chippington-Smythe?"

"Me? Nothing. Just going for a dip."

"I have always suspected you of mental instability."

Euphonia was writing busily in her notebook with an odd little smile on her face. "That was very sweet, Mr. Chippington-Smythe."

"Sweet?"

"Jumping into the river to show off for me. It was very gallant."

"Was it? I didn't mean it to be."

"The battle between you and Mr. Wickford-Davies is growing very close. You may be ahead by a tiny margin."

Cubby made a strangled little noise. "Come, sister, it is time for tea."

"Of course. Let me just get my scarf." And with that, Euphonia turned and walked off the bank and into the river.

"Euphonia!" Cubby quickly waded in and pulled her out. "What are you doing?"

She laughed gaily. "How silly of me! I forgot there was a river there. I must change my clothing."

Suddenly Bentley was there. "May I assist you, Madam?"

"Of course. Thank you, Bentley."

As Bentley led Euphonia away I caught his eye and we exchanged a meaningful glance. The plan was working perfectly. Soon the incriminating pages would be ripped from her notebook and Binky and I would be but shadows on the blank canvas of Euphonia's memory.

My satisfaction was tempered somewhat by a furious hubbub coming from the direction of the temple. My eyesight has never been my strong suit, but the hazy blobs in the distance gradually resolved themselves into my cousin Binky being hustled down the street by an angry mob. As they drew nearer, I saw that his arms were pinioned behind his back. Ahmed Ben Fitzwilliam ran up to me breathlessly.

"Alas, Sir, it is a disaster! Your cousin was caught trying to steal eggs. I'm afraid he is in a most perilous position!"

"What? You don't mean to say they arrest a fellow over a few eggs?"

"Of course, they do! If eggs are pure evil then it follows as the night the day that anyone who covets them must also be evil."

"What will they do to him?"

"He must come to trial. The penalties can be severe."

The crowd was drawing near. Binky looked rather dazed. He spotted me and struggled against his bonds to reach me.

"Help me, Cyril! It's all a misunderstanding. I never wanted any eggs. Tell them I was only doing it for you!"

Fitzwilliam whirled around to stare at me. "Is this true, Sir?"

Well, blood is blood after all. I couldn't let Binky be drawn and quartered for following my instructions. "I'm afraid so. He was but an unwitting tool. I am the guilty party. I shall pay any fine you deem appropriate."

Fitzwilliam was sweating freely now. "Alas, Sir, if only it was a fine! The penalty for stealing eggs is death!"

CHAPTER SEVEN

Crime and Punishment

Well, as you can imagine, everything went hazy for a while. People seemed to be speaking to me but it was as if I was hearing them from a great distance. Hands pulled and pushed me here and there. After what seemed like hours the world came back into focus and I found myself sitting in a courtroom handcuffed to a desk. Binky sat next to me chattering away.

"And that's why I can't eat spicy food," he said.

"What on earth are you talking about?"

He looked hurt. "Have you not been listening to me?"

"I've had a lot on my mind in case you haven't noticed."

Cubby was sitting at our table shuffling through some papers. He beckoned to a court official and they put their heads together for a moment. I tapped him with my unshackled hand.

"Where do we stand, Cubby?"

He looked grim. "The situation is not optimal, I'm afraid. Fortunately, you have me to speak in your defense."

"Do I? Am I glad of that?"

"I have been an advocate at many disciplinary hearings at the club. I think I understand this sort of thing better than most lawyers do."

"Hmm. You haven't seen Bentley about, have you?"

"I'm afraid that automatons are barred from the courtroom. He is in the square awaiting the outcome."

I peered around the courtroom and saw that my aunt and uncle were sitting in the front row, along with Cheeseworth and Euphonia. Euphonia was looking distraught and clutching at the empty place where her notebook usually hung. I managed a weak little smile. At least one thing was going to plan. Bentley undoubtedly had the notebook and was busily tearing out any references to yours truly.

Ahmed Ben Fitzwilliam, wearing a fleecy wig, sat at the judge's bench looking grim.

"Is the prosecution ready?" he asked.

A weaselly-looking fellow who I took to be the Court Recorder raised a hand. "I'm afraid the prosecutors have all managed to escape. We performed a thorough search but none could be found."

This seemed to cheer Fitzwilliam up. "And since, I presume, the defense lawyers have also vanished, these defendants have no representation, therefore I must declare a mistrial. Court is adjour..."

Before he could finish his sentence Cubby leaped to his feet. "I shall act in defense of these men, Your Honour!"

Fitzwilliam frowned. "You understand that in the event of a mistrial they would be freed on their own recognizance until a new trial could be held. If, by some chance, they should leave the vicinity, there would be little chance of bringing them back to face these charges."

"As men of honour, they refuse to live with the shame of being branded criminals. They wish to clear their reputations."

Binky looked at me. "Do we?"

I shrugged helplessly.

Fitzwilliam sighed. "Oh well, I tried."

I grabbed Cubby's sleeve and yanked. "Are you sure you know what you're doing?"

"Trust me. These country boobs are no match for me."

Fitzwilliam had continued. "In the absence of a prosecutor I shall act as both prosecutor and judge. The charges are that at the direction of Mr. Chippington-Smythe, this fellow here... Cheswick Wickford-Davies, attempted to steal half a dozen eggs."

Binky stood up. "I accept!"

Fitzwilliam peered at him. "Accept what?"

"Isn't that what they say? I know they do it in plays. When things are going badly someone always jumps up and yells, 'I accept!'"

"Do you mean that you object?"

"Is that what it is? Very well, I object."

"You object to what?"

"Everything, I suppose. It's a kind of general dissatisfaction. A kind of existential emptiness that leads one to say, 'What's it all about after all?'"

"You cannot object on the basis that life is a hollow fraud. If one could, the courts would be a shambolic carnival of objections and nothing would ever get done. Sit down."

Binky subsided with a muted, "Oh I say."

"The prosecution calls Ned Nockbottom to the stand."

The guard who had been dragging Binky down the street hopped onto the witness chair.

"Are you Ned Nockbottom?" asked Fitzwilliam.

"You know I am."

"It's just a formality. Do you swear to tell the truth?"

The guard looked hurt. "What sort of question is that? Have you ever known me to lie?"

"Again, just a formality."

"Well, I'm not the one on trial."

"Fine. We'll assume you're telling the truth."

"Assume away."

Fitzwilliam scratched under his wig and sighed. "What happened, Ned?"

"I was on duty as usual when that fellow a-setting over there comes whistling into the temple with his hands in his pockets. I thought he was acting suspicious-like, so I kept an eye on him. He strolls about through the chickens, looking up at the ceiling like he'd never seen a ceiling before. When he thought I wasn't looking, he ducked down, grabbed a few handfuls of eggs and shoved 'em in his pockets. 'Ere,' I yelled. 'Stop that.' Well, he takes off like a shot with me after him. I caught him pretty easy—he's not much of a runner. The eggs was in his pockets, so... there it is."

Fitzwilliam looked gloomy. "Seems pretty cut and dried. Does the defense have any questions?"

Cubby jumped to his feet. "No questions, Your Honour."

I stared at him. "No questions?"

"Don't worry. I have a plan."

Binky perked up. "That's usually my line."

Cubby raised his hand. "Your Honour, I ask that this case be dismissed on the grounds that my clients are members of Twits, the well-known gentlemen's club. I'm sure you are aware that the laws of the land are suspended within the walls of Twits, therefore these men must be set free."

Fitzwilliam shook his head regretfully. "As the former Hatter of Twits, I am well aware of its immunity, however we are not within the walls of Twits."

Cubby was undeterred. "A gentleman carries his club with him at all times. It envelops him like a suit of armor. Wheresoever a man of Twits stands, there too stands his club. I contend that each member is equivalent to an embassy of a foreign power, with sovereignty within the walls of his person."

My uncle jumped up from his seat in the front row with a hearty "Hear, hear!" but a glare from Fitzwilliam put the stopper in.

I have to admit, Cubby's eloquence moved me. I actually grew a bit teary thinking about the old club. Fitzwilliam was paging through an enormous book. The courtroom seemed to hold its breath. At last, he closed the book with a sigh.

"Alas, although your argument is poetic, it is not enshrined in law. Individuals are not embassies and these men must answer for their crimes."

I patted Cubby's arm. "It was a good try, Cubby."

"I'm not finished yet." He raised his hand again. "Your Honour, I would like to call a few character witnesses."

"Very well."

"I call Hypatia Dankworth to the stand."

My aunt rose and glided to the stand like an ocean liner easing up to a pier. The crowd murmured appreciatively. The court recorder approached her.

"Do you swear to tell the truth, the whole truth and nothing but the truth?"

"I do not. You ask the impossible. To tell the whole truth would be the work of years. Anyone of my acquaintance will tell you that I already tell more truth than is comfortable or necessary. I will promise to be accurate in my statements if you will promise not to aim the aromatic remains of your lunch, which must have contained obscene quantities of garlic, toward my face."

Cubby strolled toward my aunt, tapping his lips with a pen and looking thoughtful. The effect was ruined by a crooked floorboard that caused him to stagger, but he reached her at last.

"You have known the defendants for a good while, have you not?"

"I have known them since they were squalling infants. Their behavior sometimes makes me wonder if they have progressed from that stage at all."

"Have you ever known them to engage in criminal behavior before this?"

"Their crimes hitherto have been confined to offenses against good taste. They have also been guilty of ingratitude toward their loving aunt whom they seem to regard as nothing more than an endless cornucopia of favours."

"They are upstanding members of society?"

"Cyril Chippington-Smythe is the richest man in the world. On that basis alone he would be considered an upstanding member of society even if he thought he was a teapot and danced naked in Piccadilly Square. His cousin, Cheswick, who *has* danced naked in Piccadilly Square is harder to quantify."

Binky stood. "I've explained that! I wasn't meant to mix my cold medication with my aphrodisiac. Anyone could have made the same mistake."

I pulled him back into his seat. "You're only making it worse, Old Hound. Sit still like a good lad."

Cubby faced the jury and hooked his thumbs under his armpits. "In short, the idea that the defendants would engage in criminal behavior is laughable."

My aunt considered for a moment. "That depends on what you consider criminal behavior. That phrase has very different meanings depending on whether it is used by the general population or by people of quality."

Cubby slumped a little. "I am asking you to attest to the good character of these men."

"A woman of breeding should never attest to anything at any time. Taking a position merely ensures that half of your acquaintance will disagree with you. It leads to people discussing you furtively in cloakrooms which is a depth of depravity that I have worked long and hard to avoid."

Cubby knew when he was licked. "Thank you, Madam, you may step down. The defense calls C. Langford-Cheeseworth to the stand."

Cheeseworth rose and took his place in the box. Cubby gave the jury a confident smile. "Your name is C. Langford-Cheeseworth?"

Cheeseworth adjusted his monocle. "I refuse to answer on the gwounds that it may tend to incwiminate me."

Cubby stared at him, dumbfounded. "Your name is not C. Langford-Cheeseworth?"

"I did not say that."

"Then what..." Cubby made a little choking sound and started again. "How long have you known the defendants?"

"We went to school together, and have been fellow members of Twits since we achieved manhood."

"Have you ever known either of them to lie?"

"Oh, my word, yes. One can hardly have lived one's life without lying, can one?"

Cubby was turning red. "But you're speaking of the little white lies that grease one's everyday interactions, are you not? You're not talking about falsehoods deliberately designed to mislead others for one's own gain?"

Cheeseworth leaned back in the witness chair and waved his jeweled walking stick about in the air lazily.

"I don't know what you'd call it when a person forges another member's signature on an IOU in order to place a wager."

Binky jumped up again. "I accept!"

"Object," I murmured.

"Object! I only did it because it was a sure thing."

Fitzwilliam leaned forward. "That does not excuse committing forgery."

"But it didn't count because I couldn't lose! Am I the only one who sees the distinction?"

"Better leave it, Old Possum," I muttered, pulling him by the sleeve.

Cubby was openly sweating now. "Will you attest to the spotless character of the defendants?" he practically pleaded.

"Of course, dear boy! You couldn't find two finer fellows—always up for a scandalous caper or an evening of debauchery. We've spent many a night together sleeping it off at the local constabulary—but no convictions! My word, no. Spotless records, both of them."

I could see the fight had been knocked out of Cubby. He waved at Cheeseworth weakly. "You may step down."

Cheeseworth trotted back to his seat and Cubby surveyed his remaining prospects. I could see him debating with himself as to who would do us the most harm—Uncle Hugo or Euphonia, when there was a stir at the back of the courtroom. The onlookers parted and down the aisle strode Smith and Jones! They wore their ceremonial egg costumes and looked pretty grim. Smith spoke up first.

"Your Honour, we demand that this trial be suspended at once!"

Fitzwilliam stood. "On what grounds?"

Now Jones spoke up. "On the grounds that it concerns eggs, and anything to do with eggs belongs in our jurisdiction."

"But the eggs were stolen in our jurisdiction," sputtered Fitzwilliam.

Smith drew himself up. "The sanctity of eggs recognizes no borders or arbitrary divisions of men. Eggs are, were and always will be."

"Praise eggs!" shouted Jones.

Fitzwilliam rubbed his head. "We were almost done. Nothing left but the sentencing. Can't we work something out?"

Smith and Jones put their heads together and whispered for a tick. Jones finally turned to Fitzwilliam. "We agree to abide by the decision of the jury if we can choose the punishment."

Fitzwilliam rubbed his head thoughtfully. He scanned the jury, who were all giving Binky and me the fish eye pretty strongly. Finally, he nodded. "That is acceptable. Has the jury reached a verdict?"

"I wasn't finished," objected Cubby.

"Oh yes, you are. Sit down!" shouted Fitzwilliam.

The jury foreman stood. "We think they did it, all right. Plus, we just don't like the look of 'em."

"Fine. Cyril Chippington-Smythe and Cheswick Wickford-Davies, you have been found guilty of the crime of stealing eggs. I leave it to the High Eggs to pronounce sentence."

This perked me up, as you can imagine. Anything the High Eggs came up with was bound to be better than death. Smith and Jones found a beam of light that was squeezing through a crack and disposed themselves dramatically. Smith cleared his throat.

"In accordance with the universal code of Eggnostic conduct, there is no penalty for taking eggs. Such an act is unimaginable and therefore we have never considered what should be done."

I turned to Binky and beamed. "We're off the hook, Old Flounder!"

Jones picked up the narrative. "Touching sacred eggs with human hands, however, is a terrible crime. Who can say where a hand has been? I mean, hands touch all sorts of disgusting things. It makes me a little queasy to think about some of the things mine have touched. You can't paw a pristine egg with your grubby mitts. Not without serious consequences."

Smith stepped in front of her. "The penalty for touching a sacred egg with your hands, or inciting someone to touch an egg, is..."

I held my breath.

"A paddling!"

Cubby looked appalled. "A paddling? That is undignified! My clients would rather die!"

I punched him in the kidney. "Shut up, Cubby! You're fired."

Smith continued. "Twenty strokes with the paddle of justice in the town square should balance the scales... and since everyone will be gathered together to witness the punishment, after the paddling is complete my partner and I will entertain the crowd by performing,

'The Misadventures of Barnaby Fudge, Boy Pharmacist.'"

Fitzwilliam slammed his gavel. "Court Adjourned!"

The spectators streamed from the courtroom and into the square. Binky and I were hustled onto a raised platform with a large log lying upon it. Our arms were tied behind us. An enormous fellow wearing a black hood stood holding an ax.

"Hold on," I croaked. "This is only supposed to be a paddling."

The executioner sheepishly hid his ax under the platform. "Sorry, Sir. I needed it to chop down that there log. Here's what we're after." He pulled out an enormous, wicked-looking paddle. "This is Old Betsy."

In my youthful school days, it was rumoured that the headmaster had a paddle which was capable of delivering astonishing blows. It was said that he had placed holes at strategic points to improve its aerodynamics and that he could be seen in the dead of night sitting in his office polishing it with beeswax and crooning to it softly. No one ever actually saw it but the rumour of its existence strangled many a youthful plot in its crib. Here was my nightmare, come to life at last.

My hindquarters began to vibrate in anticipation.
I closed my eyes and prayed for sweet oblivion.

Chapter Eight

Many Escapes

I have sometimes wondered what stirring words I might utter in a crisis. I assumed that the old noodle would rise to the occasion with something along the lines of, "It is a far, far better thing," etcetera, but the moment was at hand and the only thing I seemed to be capable of saying was, "Well, well, well."

Bentley appeared at my elbow. "Excuse me, Sir, but your garments are somewhat the worse for wear. A gentleman should never appear before a bloodthirsty mob looking *dishabille*."

He proceeded to brush, poke and prod me vigorously. He then turned to Binky and performed a similar transformation. I must say, he was right. I felt fortified against the humiliation that was to come.

Binky and I were forced to our knees and bent over the log in the center of the platform. The executioner, who had stripped to the waist, took a few practice swings with his paddle. I turned to Binky.

"Courage, Old Sack!"

"Oh, I'm not afraid. Don't you remember? I lost all feeling in my backside from being caned so frequently as a youth. It's damned inconvenient on the loo, as you can imagine, but it comes in handy at times like this."

"Well, that doesn't seem fair!"

"It is too! I've spent most of my life sliding off of benches and sitting on thumb tacks. It's about time my infirmity worked to my advantage."

Fitzwilliam stepped forward. "Do you have any last words before the sentence is carried out?"

"Yes! Yes, I do!" I practically shouted. Anything to delay the inevitable. Unfortunately, my mind was still blank. I struggled to my feet and stared out at the crowd. They looked back at me rather hungrily.

"Well, well, well," I began. "It's awfully good of all of you to turn out like this. Most gratifying I must say. Yes, if a fellow has to be paddled to within an inch of his life it certainly helps to have the support of his fellow citizens."

"Get on with it!" yelled someone in the crowd.

"Smack 'em good!"

"Don't you go easy on 'em, Hank! Give 'em something to remember!"

It seems I had misjudged the sentiment of the crowd. Binky stepped up beside me.

"You ought to be ashamed of yourselves," he declared. "I don't speak for myself, for I am a man and am indifferent to pain, but this poor fellow..." Here he plopped a hand on my shoulder and bestowed a pitying look on me. "This poor, pampered soul has never known suffering. His lily-white skin has never been blemished by the cruel strokes of the lash. Have some pity, in the name of God!"

There was a moment of silence and then a large, rotting cabbage came arcing through the air and caught Binky square in the chest. He turned to me. "Well, I tried. Good luck."

We were bent over the log. It is possible that a tiny whimper escaped me. As the executioner raised his paddle there was a sudden gasp from the crowd. I felt an odd, pecking sensation from the area destined for punishment. The pecking continued and still the paddle did not fall. There was a sudden shout.

"It's a sign!"

"Praise chickens!"

I turned my head to look at Binky but he just shrugged. I craned my neck. "I say, what's going on back there?"

Fitzwilliam jumped up onto the platform. "My friends, the message is clear—this sacred chicken has interposed herself between these men and the paddle of justice! She herself has administered the symbolic peck of punishment. They have paid for their crime and must be released!"

A great shout arose from the crowd. Our arms were untied and I could at last look behind me. I found Cackles industriously pecking at my backside. I leaned down to pat her feathery head.

"Well, it seems you've saved our bacon, Old Girl."

There was a shout from the crowd. "Ain't nobody going to get smacked?"

A low grumble rose from the villagers. Fitzwilliam raised his arms for silence.

"My friends, you forget, there is still the sentence on the lawyer to be carried out!"

Cubby whirled around. "I beg your pardon?"

"Perhaps I should have mentioned it sooner, but lawyers are held in rather low esteem here. It is a lucrative profession, but the price for that exalted income is that the losing lawyer in every case is punished along with their clients. It improves their efforts in the courtroom immeasurably although they have become increasingly skilled at camouflage."

"But... you don't mean you're going to paddle me?"

"Oh, no Sir. The punishment for the lawyer is much less severe. To the manure pit, everyone!"

"To the what?" Cubby gave an anguished cry but he was seized by the guards and hustled across the square to a large pit which, upon examination, proved to be full of chicken droppings, feathers and grass clippings.

"Let justice be done!" cried Fitzwilliam.

Cubby was flung into the air and landed with a resounding splat. He lay, stunned, and the crowd, having hooted its appreciation, drifted away to rehash the day's events.

Cubby emerged from the pile of grass and chicken droppings. They clung to him and formed a luxurious green moustache. Binky stared at him.

"Do you know who you look like with that moustache? You look exactly like that fellow that won the Delivery Persons' Race. What was his name?"

My uncle stepped forward and stared at Cubby. "Mario Grubenspieler... and you don't just <u>look</u> like him... you *are* him!"

Cheeseworth adjusted his monocle. "My word! So he is. But you are not a delivery person, so you were not eligible to participate in the Delivery Persons' Race."

Cubby had been frantically scraping the foul-smelling clippings from his person. Now he drew himself up haughtily. "As it happens, I have been a delivery person in good standing since I was seventeen."

I frowned. "But how can that be when you are the Marshall of Twits?"

"It must be inconceivable to someone of your privileged position to imagine that a person would have to work at two jobs to make ends meet."

"Why don't you ask the club for a salary increase? I'll put in a good word."

"The position of Club Marshall is an honorary one. I draw no compensation for performing my duties."

"You do it for free?"

"I have the satisfaction of contributing to an institution that I hold in the highest regard. But a person must eat."

"So you moonlight as a delivery person. But why the disguise?"

"My deliveries are often at the homes of club members. I do not wish to have my authority eroded, hence the false moustache."

"How did you come up with Mario Grubenspieler?"

"Grubenspieler was my mother's name before she married Otto Martinez."

"And Mario?"

"Cubby is a nickname. My given name is Mario."

"So you had every right to participate in the Delivery Persons' Race."

"I have been a participant for years. This is the first year I have been fortunate enough to win."

"But it was a cheat! Ernie was nobbled," exclaimed Binky.

"Not by me! I had nothing to do with it. I ran a fair race and was declared the winner."

I frowned. "But if you didn't sabotage Ernie then who did, and why?"

At this point Euphonia, who had been wandering aimlessly about the square finally joined us. She stared at Cubby and gave a sudden hoot of laughter. "Cubby! What are you playing at? You smell terrible."

Bentley gave a little cough. "I'm sorry to interrupt, Sir, but I have located Miss Gumboot's missing notebook and I'm sure she is very anxious to have it returned to her."

He produced the item and passed it over to Euphonia, who clutched it thankfully and looped the cord over her head so that it hung in its accustomed place.

Binky wriggled excitedly. "I say, Euphonia. Is there anything in there about me? You know, anything of a personal nature that might indicate the status of our relationship, on... say... page sixteen?"

She quickly riffled through the pages. "Oh yes! Here it is." She read for a moment then looked up at Binky brightly. "Why, Mr. Wickford-Davies, you are terribly in love with me!"

Binky looked as if someone had caught him in the back of the head with something heavy. "What? That's still in there?" He looked at Bentley with a wounded expression. "I thought perhaps... there might have been... an updated version of events. Excuse me one moment."

He grabbed Bentley by one arm and I took the other. We walked him a few steps away and huddled together.

"Look here," I whispered hoarsely, "You were supposed to tear that bit out, weren't you? What have you been doing with that notebook all this time?"

He looked back at us placidly. "I could not remove the relevant page for the simple reason that there was an entry on the other side of the page that it was necessary to preserve." He turned back to Euphonia. "Would you please read the entry on page fifteen, Miss Gumboot?"

Euphonia flipped to the previous page and began to read. "Cubby looks very funny in his wig and false moustache. I mustn't tease him, though. He is overly sensitive about such things. I'm sure he will win, especially as I removed the cotter pins from the wheels of the race favourite."

Bentley interrupted her. "Thank you, Miss. That is all we needed to hear."

There was a profound silence as we all stared at Euphonia. Cubby was frozen. His eyes bulged. Finally, he stuttered, "You did wh-what?"

Euphonia frowned at him. "Apparently I removed the pins that hold the wheels on. You never would have won otherwise. He was much faster than you. His name was... let me see..." She looked back at her book. "Ernie or some such. He looked like a very nice young man. I hope he is all right."

Cubby had turned bright red. "But Euphonia, that's cheating!"

"It was only a little trophy," she pooh-poohed. "You wanted it so badly."

Cubby looked around him. "I am humiliated beyond measure. I shall inform the club stewards at once. They will disqualify me. The second-place finisher will be declared the winner."

Binky snapped upright. "That's Ernie! I win! You see, Cyril, I told you it was a sure thing! Null and his daughter can go whistle for it."

"I shall also resign my position as Club Marshall. I am not morally fit to hold the office."

I watched Cubby deflate. True, he was the bane of my existence, but it was painful to watch his humiliation.

"Listen, Cubby, none of this was your fault. There's no reason anyone has to know that you and Grubenspieler are one and the same. All that matters is that the rightful winner is acknowledged. Let me talk to the trustees. They're all mates of mine. Besides, where could we find someone besides you who would do the job for nothing?"

"But what of Euphonia?"

"When they understand her unique... situation, I'm sure they'll be compassionate enough to conceal her involvement. What would be the point of punishing her for something she doesn't remember doing?"

Cubby looked like a man locked in an interior struggle for supremacy. Finally, he slumped. "I would be extremely grateful for your assistance, Sir."

"Not at all. It's the least I can do."

He looked up into my eyes. There was a hint of mania in their coffee-coloured depths. "Do not deceive yourself into thinking that anything has changed between us. If I am to remain the Marshall of Twits then you will receive no special consideration from me. If anything, I will hold you to a higher standard than ever."

"I would expect no less, Cubby, my lad." The world tilted back onto its accustomed axis and I breathed a sigh of relief.

CHAPTER NINE

The Egg and I

Back on the land yacht I sipped a cup of the old Lapsang Souchong while Bentley removed layers of unspeakable things from my shoes. The rest of the party were slumped with exhaustion about the cabin and were weakly calling for tea.

I leaned over to Bentley and murmured quietly, "All things considered, our journey turned out rather well."

"I'm glad you are pleased, Sir."

"Of course, there's still the matter of Euphonia."

Bentley set down my shoes and turned to look at the party in question, who was turning pages in her book and quietly moving her lips as she read odd passages. "Pardon me, Miss Gumboot, but Mr. Chippington-Smythe is anxious to know where he stands in the competition for your affections."

This startled me, as you can imagine. I couldn't think what Bentley was playing at. He seemed to be throwing fuel on a very nasty fire. Binky bolted up in his chair with his hair practically standing on end.

"Let's not press the lady," he stuttered.

Euphonia happily turned to the last entry in her notebook and read silently for a moment. Her face fell. "It seems that I found both of my suitors lacking. Apparently, I informed them that their attentions were no longer welcome. I hope you are not too disappointed."

Binky and I stared at her, then turned and stared at Bentley. I was the first to regain the power of speech.

"Not at all. Absolutely right! Couple of rotters. Don't deserve you in the slightest. Think nothing of it!"

Euphonia gave a satisfied smile. "Oh, I won't. I am actually unclear as to what we are talking about but I assure you that I harbour no ill will toward any living creature. Tea!" She squealed and clapped her hands.

Cook had entered with a steaming pot of the elixir and began to busily distribute cups and saucers. I looked at Bentley inquiringly.

"How came this miracle to manifest?"

He gave a little bow. "Among my talents is the ability to mimic handwriting with a high degree of accuracy. I simply added an entry to Miss Gumboot's notebook that has achieved the desired effect."

"Brilliant!:" I was struck by an uncomfortable thought. "I say, do you mimic *my* handwriting?"

"Frequently, Sir. You rarely answer your correspondence."

I digested this for a moment. "I suppose that's all right then." I leaned back in my chair. "What an adventure this has been, eh, Bentley? How do you suppose Smith and Jones knew about the trial?"

"I managed to get a message to them. I emphasized that they were very much in your debt for your generous gesture in releasing them from your employment. I am pleased that they responded as they did."

"Thank you, Bentley. Very shrewd. There's one thing you can't take credit for though—Cackles coming to my rescue like that. It just goes to show that animals have feelings like anyone else."

"I am certain that they do, Sir, but in this instance, I fear there was a more mundane explanation."

"What do you mean?"

"I noted that corn was Cackles's food of choice and so I placed a quantity of corn in your back pockets and in those of Mr. Wickford-Davies. I rightly presumed that the corn would draw her to the area that had been marked for punishment and that the court would be loath to disturb her by carrying out the sentence."

"Did you, by Jove? When did you do it? I don't recall anything being stuffed in my pockets."

"It was while I was brushing your clothes to prepare you for the ordeal. I have a great deal of manual dexterity and have made a study of the art of pickpocketing— in order to forestall such a crime, of course. The knowledge does occasionally come in handy."

I reached into my back pockets and brought out handfuls of golden corn kernels. "I must say, Bentley, you're an absolute wizard."

"I am undeserving of praise, Sir. Any schoolboy could have thought of it."

A squawk from beneath my chair revealed that Cackles had followed us onto the land yacht and was making herself at home. She jumped up to seize some corn from my hand. I scattered the rest onto the floor which she quickly pecked up.

"Well, this is awkward. What do you think we should do? Should we return her to her fellows at the temple?"

Bentley considered for a moment. "Life in the Temple Pullum may not be the chicken paradise that the locals believe it is. If Cackles wishes to accompany us I'm sure that I can make her comfortable in the garden behind the house."

Having scoured the area for stray corn kernels, Cackles finally made herself at home in the corner where Compton and his family had made a comfy pile of straw. I bent down to look her in the eye.

"Are you sure you want to come with us, Old Girl? You would be leaving your fellow chickens forever. Won't you be lonely?"

Cackles gave a squawk and settled herself more deeply into the straw. She stared back at me defiantly.

"Well then, it seems we are not leaving empty handed after all."

Uncle Hugo's face did something disquieting and I realized that he was smiling. The necessary musculature had almost atrophied from disuse and he couldn't hold it for long, but the sight of it haunted my dreams for some years after.

"This could not have worked out better! She will begin a flock which, if carefully managed, will increase in number exponentially. The revenue stream from this enterprise will be enormous! We shall have a monopoly on the sale of eggs and processed chickens."

I looked down at Cackles. She looked at me. A vision rose up before me of Cackles and her descendants crammed into a new Temple Pullum with Uncle Hugo standing over them cracking a whip and chortling maniacally. It may have been my imagination, but I fancied I saw a tiny tear run down her beak.

Bentley cranked the autopilot a few times and the land yacht began its glide to freedom. We were passing the temple when I noticed that the guards were conspicuously absent.

"I say, Bentley, could you pause for a moment?"

He massaged the controls and we glided to a stop.

"Why are we lingering in this savage locale?" inquired my aunt.

"I'm just wondering where the guards are?"

Uncle Hugo consulted his watch. "It is time for the evening ceremony. I presume they are all at the bridge."

Binky looked at me curiously. "What are you planning?"

"Wait here." I hopped down from the land yacht and raced to the door of the temple. Seizing the door knob, I gave a mighty heave but it was locked up tight. I trotted back to the yacht.

"Bentley, do we have a piece of stout rope?"

"Of course, Sir."

He rummaged in a cupboard and brought out a coil of hempen line. I raced back to the door of the temple and tied one end tightly to the door knob. It was the work of a moment to affix the other end to the rear of the land yacht.

"All right, give it a little pull, Bentley"

The line grew taut. The door groaned and then the entire front wall of the temple slowly separated from the structure and majestically descended in a cloud of dust. There was a moment of absolute silence as thousands of pairs of chicken eyes stared at me, and then the temple erupted in pandemonium. With a roar, a wave of frenzied poultry headed straight for me. I covered my eyes and prepared to meet my maker, but the tsunami parted around me and the Chippington-Smythe line was preserved for another day.

The temple was empty as the flock scrambled for freedom, clucking and flapping in a most satisfactory way—all but one. Cackles had followed me off the land yacht and stood before me. She looked at me curiously, her head cocked to one side. She turned to watch her fellows disappear into the forest and then turned back to me. She took a step toward me, looked me dead in the eye, squatted down in the dust and, with a triumphant squawk, laid an egg. She stepped to one side, looked at the egg, looked at me, turned and walked after her compatriots. I watched her until the underbrush had swallowed her up, then tenderly lifted her last gift to me and carried it in my cupped palms to the land yacht.

It was late in the evening. Everyone else was deep in slumber. I stared down at the plate that Cook had set before me. A golden orb wobbled atop a shining white disk with just a little brown around the edges. I carefully pierced the orb with a tine of my fork and the golden essence within oozed onto the white. I sliced off a corner and carefully lifted it to my mouth. Cook watched me intently as I chewed.

"It's absolutely delicious," I finally declared. "Such an improvement on cheesy eggs. No comparison."

She exhaled. "Well, that's a relief and no mistake. I don't know how many recipes I tried before I came up with that one. The secret is black salt. It has a touch of sulfur that really tastes like the eggs I remember."

I sighed. "Yes, it's the best imitation egg I've ever tasted. Perhaps we should manufacture them. Shame to keep it to ourselves."

She gazed at me sympathetically. "No regrets?"

"No. I couldn't eat Cackles' egg. I'd feel like a cannibal."

"I think you acted very nobly. Some of the things we did before the Great Extinction seem barbaric when you think back on them. Perhaps if we had a second chance, we'd be kinder to other species. If we'd been a little more thoughtful there might not have been a Great Extinction at all."

"You may be right, Cook. Do you know, I'm a little tired. Lot of excitement today. I think I'll toddle off to bed." I scraped up the last bit from the plate and let it melt on my tongue.

"Good night, dear. Sleep well."

As I stepped into my sleeping compartment I looked up and down the corridor. Seeing no one, I gently closed the door and padded over to the bed. There, swaddled in a pair of my flannel pajamas with a hot water bottle next to it, was Cackles' egg. I gazed at it fondly for a moment, carefully crouched down and settled myself atop it, being careful not to crush the delicate little thing. I sat happily on my charge and began to hum a little nursery rhyme I remembered from childhood. As I hummed, new lyrics came crowding into my brain.

"Twinkle, twinkle little egg,
Lying warm beneath my leg.
Though we've caused the earth to fry,
I won't let your species die.
Twinkle, twinkle little egg
Give us one more chance. I beg."

The End

If you enjoyed this book, please
take a moment to visit
Amazon and provide a short
review; every reader's voice is
extremely important for the life
of a book or series.

If you'd like advance notice on the next book's
release head to:
WWW.TwitsChronicles.com
where you can sign up for my email list and where
you can ask Cyril and his friends a question which
they may choose to answer in a newsletter.
I hate spam as much as you do, so I will keep
emails to a minimum.

**Cyril, Bentley and The Usual Suspects will
return in:**

TWITS TO THE TEST

The next installment of The Twits Chronicles.
Read on for a taste:

I did not wish to live.

"Bentley," I managed to croak, "Help!"

Charles Barnswoggle is a git. I say it, and I stand by it. It was he who had introduced the gang to something called a "mai tai" at the club the previous evening. Now the rosy beams of the inevitable morning found me locked in a paroxysm of pain that made all previous hangovers seem like hangnails. I hazily recalled a limbo contest, breaking glass and gigantic teeth giving one the hee-haw.

"Bentley?" I lay still and waited for the dependable entrance of my mechanical valet. There would be aspirin and hair of the dog. Bentley would save me. Minutes passed and the only thing that danced attendance were the dust motes in the sunbeams. Comprehension suddenly burst through the alcoholic fog. An icy hand grasped my vitals. I had forgotten that this was the one day of the year when Bentley returned to the factory for an overhaul. I was alone!

You will observe, quite rightly, that I should have been prepared. The date had been circled by Bentley on a large calendar which he had hung by my bedside the previous evening.

"You will recall, Sir, that I shall not be here to attend on you tomorrow?"

"Yes, yes, Bentley. I shall be quite all right."

"May I suggest once again that you forgo any carousing at the club tonight? I will not be in a position to post bail or to suture any wounds you may receive."

"Good heavens, I'm not a child. I'm quite capable of taking care of myself."

I had spoken with all the confidence of youth, but my cousin Binky had convinced me that there was nothing sinister about a little game of bridge in the card room. Barnswoggle had turned up with those misbegotten mai tais and here I was.

Think... I must think! I squinted at the clock on the wall—seven fifty-nine. The morning cannons would thunder forth in one minute! I knew from past hangovers how devastating their reverberations could be.

"Steady, Old Boy," I murmured to myself. Moving at a glacial pace, I extended a shaking arm and managed to hook a nearby pillow. I laboriously dragged it toward me and pulled it over my head just as the cannons up and down the road went off with a roar! Despite the muting

effects of the poly-fill, the pain was indescribable!
I breathed deeply and managed to slow the old
ticker. First crisis averted. Now, what to do about
my swelling bladder?

I was just reaching out a claw to grasp the
blanket when I heard the front doorbell. I had
been convinced by a fast-talking salesperson that
musical doorbells were going to be all the rage this
season but was growing devilishly tired of hearing
"Lady of Spain" every time someone yanked the
cord. Whoever was at the door wouldn't take no
for a bloody answer. "Lady of Spain" must have
played through five or six times before a blessed
silence fell—then, to my horror, I heard the front
door creak! I heard footsteps on the stairs! The
bedroom door slowly opened and who should
enter the boudoir but my Aunt Hypatia! Well, this
was too much. I closed my eyes and gave myself
up for lost.

"There you are, Nephew. What are you doing
in bed? The morning cannons have sounded. Live
free or die."

My aunt's voice has been compared to a
trumpet. I would have said a steam whistle on a
tugboat, but I am not impartial.

"Can't speak, Aunt... sick."

"Sick? Nonsense. Wellness is an act of will! You must will yourself out of bed and you will see how much better you feel."

"Can't move... hurts."

"Where does it hurt?"

"Everywhere."

She came nearer and peered at me intently. She sniffed suspiciously. "Have you been drinking?"

"Not at all. Perhaps I had a beer."

"The alcohol is positively leaking out of your pores. You have a hangover."

"It is possible."

"Your Uncle Hugo used to suffer from that condition. I cured him of it. He has not touched a drop in twenty years."

"Poor Uncle," I murmured sympathetically, while recalling that same uncle with a mai tai in each fist at the club the previous evening.

"Don't feel sorry for him. He feels sorry enough for himself."

There was something nagging at me from a far corner of what remained of my mind. I looked up at my aunt suspiciously. "I say, Aunt, how did you get in? Bentley would never have left the front door unlocked."

"Of course not. I have a key."

I sputtered a bit. "What ho? How did you acquire such a thing?"

"I have had it for years. Your parents gave it to me before they departed. They asked me to keep an eye on you."

The mention of my parents caused me to sink deeper into my pillows. "That was thoughtful. They must have had a premonition of their impending demise."

My Aunt started and stared at me strangely. "Demise, you say?"

"Yes—how I wish they were still here to see the man I have become."

She avoided my gaze and stared at the china figurines on the nightstand. "Did Bentley tell you of their... egress?"

"He did, when I was old enough to comprehend it."

"What did he say, exactly?"

"That they were departed."

"Yes, that is undeniably accurate. You're certain that he did not say that they 'had' departed?"

"'Were', 'had', they are much the same thing. You're acting rather oddly, Aunt. Is there something you wish to tell me?"

She regained her equilibrium. "No, no... well, since I'm here, is there anything I can do to assist you?"

"You couldn't help me up, could you? I need to use the... um... facility."

"Why don't I find a bowl that you could use as a bedpan?"

"I think not."

"I have experience. During the war I held many a bedpan. I have always thought it was excellent training for serving punch at cricket matches—the cut crystal bowl with all that liquid sloshing about... ah, memories."

"Perhaps another time. If you could just remove the bedclothes from atop me and give me a boost, I think I could make it on my own."

"Very well."

She peeled back the linens with a surprisingly gentle touch and took my hand. I have always suspected that Aunt Hypatia lifts weights when no one is watching and, indeed, she pulled me to my feet like I was a kitten.

"Thanks awfully." I tottered to the bathroom, did the necessary and returned to find her holding a brimming cup that looked surprisingly familiar. "I say, is that..."

"Bentley's morning after concoction. I found it under the shirt that you had flung so cavalierly onto the dresser. There was a note. It said, "In case of emergencies.""

"'Give me. Tell me not of fear.'" I seized the glass and downed it in one gulp. My headache began to fade away and the room ceased to spin.

"Do you know," my aunt mused, "I rather miss taking care of someone. Hugo is so self-sufficient. Would you like me to make you something to eat?"

"You can cook?" I couldn't have been more amazed if she had risen into the air and flown about the room.

"Of course I can cook. I didn't always have servants."

"Didn't you?"

"The family thought that young people should learn to be self-reliant. We weren't allowed servants until we reached the age of twelve. I can heat packaged dinners and even construct the occasional sandwich."

"You're full of surprises."

She eyed me with amusement. "Not quite the dragon you imagined me to be?"

"Not at all. I say, this is rather jolly. What brought you to mi casa on this particular morning?"

Her eyes suddenly skittered away from mine and she became fascinated by the plaster moldings around the doorway. "Oh... nothing really. I did want to ask a teensy favour..."

I felt a tingle at the back of my neck that invariably signaled approaching danger. "Oh? Pray tell, what is this service that you require?"

"Well... I would very much appreciate it if you would sponsor your cousin Caspar Haspenhausen for membership at the club."

"Who, Caspar the Delinquent Ghost?" I stared at her in shock. "The members would never forgive me! Don't ask it of me, Aunt, please!"

She rose from her chair and towered over me. "What is wrong with Caspar? His lineage is every bit as elevated as your own."

"But he's a cyst, Aunt. You know he is! He's famous for disappearing whenever a bill is due and his idea of fun would embarrass a drunken Visigoth. I've lost count of the times Bentley has had to bail him out of the pokey for knocking down some poor unsuspecting police person or for heckling a parson during his Easter sermon."

"Youthful spirits!"

"Spirits are certainly at fault."

"He is your cousin. That trumps all of his supposed flaws."

"Why can't Uncle Hugo sponsor him? He's a member."

"There are procedural reasons, which your uncle has explained to me."

I suddenly saw a glimmer of hope. "But Aunt, Caspar can't be a member, you know. He's not a firstborn son."

For those of you unfamiliar with the bylaws of my club, Twits, a new member must be the firstborn son of an existing member. This may seem overly restrictive but the benefits of club membership are so overwhelming that if it were open to all and sundry there would be a tidal wave of applicants that would swamp our little paradise.

I lay back and wallowed in self-satisfaction. Bentley could not have handled it more neatly. My aunt, however, showed no signs of retreat.

"You are aware that Twits was founded by your great-great-grandfather, Percy Chippington-Smythe?"

"Yes, bless him—founder of the family fortune."

"Your uncle has explained to me that in the club charter Percy reserved certain unique powers for himself."

"Did he? He must have been a Byzantine sort of fellow."

"What you are perhaps unaware of is that these unique powers pass down through his male line."

"Do they? Most interesting," I yawned.

"The current representative of that male line is... you."

"Yes, I quite see that. Thank you for explaining."

"And among the unique powers that you possess is the power to open the membership of Twits to individuals who do not meet the criteria set forth in the charter."

This seemed to be taking an unfortunate turn. "Sorry, wha-what?" I stammered.

"Simply put, you are the only person with the power to nominate your cousin Caspar for membership."

TWITS was originally produced and distributed by Dori Berinstein, Alan Seales and the Broadway Podcast Network - the premier digital storytelling destination for everyone, everywhere who loves theatre and the performing arts. BPN.fm/Twits.

About The Author

Born in Canton Ohio and raised in a box made out of ticky-tacky, Tom Alan Robbins spent his youth as a middle-aged character actor. He has appeared in nine Broadway shows, including *The Lion King* in which he created the role of Pumbaa. He recently received a Grammy nomination for the cast album of *Little Shop of Horrors*. He has maintained a parallel career as a writer, penning scripts for TV shows like *Coach* and writing plays, one of which (*Muse*) won the New Works of Merit Playwriting Competition.

The Twits Chronicles series is his first attempt at novel writing and it has been a pure joy. He hopes to keep creating adventures for Cyril and

Bentley as long as there are readers who enjoy them.

Also By Tom Alan Robbins

THE TWITS CHRONICLES:

Twits in Love

Twits in Peril

Twits Abroad

Twits on the Loose

Twits on the Hunt

Twits to the Test

Twits on the Stump

Twits Hit the Target

The Twits Chronicles: Anthology #1

www.ingramcontent.com/pod-product-compliance
Lightning Source LLC
Chambersburg PA
CBHW060935120626
46557CB00003B/1000